GAVIN NOBLE MILLS

Harmony's Betrayal

The C6 Chronicles: Book One

To Fiona and Nadia, for rekindling my imagination.

Contents

Preface

Welcome to my latest work! I'm thrilled to have you here. To stay up to date on future releases and get access to behind-the-scenes content, click here to sign up for my newsletter, or use the URL below:

subscribepage.io/Hgt1wv

Chapter 1

Considering he was facing a minor infraction at best, Johril's stress readings were so high, one would think think he'd just murdered someone.

"Mr. Kaela, you're sweating like a pig at a barbecue. What's the problem? You're looking at a CiVal penalty of 0.2 at most, and no rehab," I said, trying to calm him down. CiVal signified a citizen's "worth" to their CiviLibran society, and more importantly, how much they would receive as a wage.

"You look like you want to hit me," Johril said shakily. He could barely make eye contact with me and had spent most of my visit staring at a spot on the floor directly in front of him.

Truthfully, I had no ill will toward the man, and I'm sure he was just reacting to my so-called resting bitch face. That, along with my ninety-fifth percentile height and weight, heavily muscled frame, and long head scar (which I kept defiantly exposed by shaving that side of my skull), had always had a generally emasculating effect on a lot of men, but was actually a great filter for determining which ones I definitely wanted nothing to do with.

"Let's run through this from start to finish," I said. "You'd been managing an education center for roughly ten years, following every rule to a tee. Then, two years ago, you hacked one of the core modules, reducing the required learning period by half, which essentially allowed you to graduate twice the number of students per given period of time. Is that correct?"

"Yes, that is correct," Johril responded sulkily, still refusing to make eye contact with me.

I assumed that running through these details would cause his cortisol and adrenaline levels to bump up, or at least affect his heart rate and breathing patterns, but they were all pretty maxed out already and had barely changed since my initial readings.

"Please explain how you did that."

"It wasn't too hard, to be honest," Johril began reluctantly. "Once I hacked into the module, I removed every second submodule, adjusted the testing questions to ignore the missing sections, and changed the submodule completion check to be via percent complete rather than total number complete," Johril explained, sweating profusely and clearly wanting to be anywhere but here.

Wow, this had to be the most boring crime I had investigated in some time, and that was saying something. If it wasn't for the unsettling way this man was acting, I probably would have fallen asleep by now.

"Mr. Kaela, I'm going to ask you again, what is causing you so much stress? And please don't say it's me this time. I can tell there is something else going on here."

"I ... well, it's just my first time going through something like this," was all he offered.

Since I was getting nowhere, I decided to put in a memory analysis request for Johril with LibraAI, the big, arrogant, artificial brain behind maintaining balance within CiviLibra's CiVal system. While that type of analysis wouldn't provide an overly trustworthy view of Johril's recent experiences, it would certainly be better than what I was getting from him at the moment.

Searching through the contacts on my heads-up display (HUD) while heading out into the hall, I found Libra, and over my built-in comm said, "LibraAI, requesting 168-hour memory analysis for citizen Johril Kaela, ID183284865. His stress levels are far above what is reasonable for a citizen who has not been involved in a traumatic, possibly violent situation."

After waiting several seconds before responding, which I suspected Libra was just doing for effect, it replied, "Request from Detective Freya Blackwood is denied. Citizen Kaela is considered low risk, and as such, valuable computing resources will continue to be prioritized for other, more important tasks." Typical.

If this had been a more serious scenario, say for example, if Libra were to notice several citizens in close proximity suddenly exhibit the telltale signs of a life-threatening situation—spiking heart and respiration rates, high stress hormone levels, increasing blood glucose levels, etc.—it would have initiated its own analysis automatically, including live monitoring of visual and auditory data, then followed that up by requesting arrest warrants. In this case, since Johril had been misbehaving for some time and had not shown any of those markers until just before I showed up, I was probably going to be on my own. Also, his crime was remarkably benign.

I knew it would not do any good to waste more time pleading with this uppity sociopath, so I decided to tap my best resource at the office, and endless well of favors, Trace Holloway. Detective Holloway and I went back a long way, spending years together in the Defense Division (DD), where I had once heroically saved his life (hence the endless well of favors).

Over my comm, I said, "Trace, I need a favor."

"Of course you do," Trace replied. "By the way, how far off am I from repaying the crushing debt I owe you?"

"Well, considering your life is priceless, I am guessing never."

"Ha! Well, in that case, how can I assist my favorite creditor?" Trace offered sarcastically.

"I am currently working an extremely boring, insignificant fraud case on citizen ID183284865. It's the kind of case that makes you want to just pack it all up and move out into the wilderness."

"You're really not getting me motivated to help you here," Trace cut in. "Plus, you talk about running off and living in the woods all the time, so I'm not sure what your point is."

I continued, ignoring his comment. "Anyway, the weird thing is, despite looking at a mere infraction, the citizen's stress hormone levels are through the roof, and his heart rate hasn't dipped below 145 since I arrived. I put in a memory analysis request with Libra because I think there is something else going on, but you can probably guess how that went. I was hoping you could put in a word with the good captain and have him place an order to force Libra off its lazy ass and get this done as soon as possible."

"You could ask him yourself, you know," Trace countered.

"You know very well how that would go," I responded. Captain Tavas and me didn't have the best working relationship, if I was being honest. I attributed it to the whole "feeling emasculated around me" thing, and definitely not the "concerning levels of insubordination" thing that he pushed back with.

"All right," Trace sighed. "Give me five minutes."

Walking back in the apartment, I noticed that Johril was now looking even more anxious, and I caught him glancing at the other side of the room.

I went over to where he had been glancing and quickly peeked in the rooms there. Nothing seemed out of the ordinary.

"What were you looking at?" I asked.

"My cat just startled me." Sure enough, as soon as he said that, a cat came darting out of the bedroom.

While waiting to hear back from Trace, I wandered over to one of the apartment windows and gazed out at the distant northeastern mountains. It didn't take me long to start wishing I was out there, instead of here with Johril.

That particular area held an important place in my heart, being host to some of my most cherished early life memories with my father. He had taught me most of my wilderness survival skills, and maybe most importantly, how to eat well and enjoy myself while out there.

"You do any camping, Johril?" I asked, trying to distract him.

"A bit, when I was a kid."

"How about up in that area?" I asked, pointing vaguely.

"Never. Have you?" This was good, he was starting to engage a bit.

"Yeah, it's one of my favorite spots, actually. I can still remember the first time I camped up there, clear as day. I was around five years old. My father and I hiked up along that river you can just make out, to a nice spot overlooking the valley below. It was autumn, and the alpine forest had that crisp, pleasing smell of damp moss and fallen leaves, which married perfectly with the wood smoke from our crackling campfire."

"You describe it very beautifully," said Johril. I glanced back to see if he was being sarcastic, but he appeared genuine. So, I continued, returning my gaze to the mountains.

"We spent the late morning foraging in the forest and small clearings and brought in a bountiful haul of maitake mushrooms, wild garlic bulbs, and huge buttery pine nuts. In the afternoon, I watched my father hunt with his goshawk, Whisper, who brought down three fat pheasants, showing off his impressive stealth and maneuverability skills in among the mature trees."

At this, I looked back at Johril and said, "Just so we're clear, I am not referring to my father here. That man had all the grace of a baby giraffe dancing on ice." This actually made Johril laugh.

"Why use a hawk?" he asked.

"Since projectile weapons are illegal, falconing has actually been used in hunting since way back when the pioneers arrived," I explained. It wasn't surprising that he didn't know this. Hardly anyone on CiviLibra6 hunted these days.

I continued what I hoped was a relaxing story. "Anyway, we spent a quiet late afternoon cooking our bounty and listening to the river bubbling away below us. Then that night, we sat in our tent watching the crackling fire, and listening to an owl hooting up in the canopy. It's funny, there's nothing really remarkable about that day, but I can walk through the whole experience as if I am there."

"I think experiences like that ground us," responded Johril. "They remind us of what's most important to us, which might be why your mind spends so much effort keeping the details intact." I nodded at this. It was a nice way to think about it.

Our story time was interrupted by Trace. "Freya, are you there?"

"Yes. How did it go?"

"Poorly, as you might have expected," Trace responded. "Maybe it's time to just move on, my friend."

"Maybe you're right," I said. "Probably just overthink—" Suddenly my comm connection dropped out.

At the same time, I felt intense pain at the base of my spine, followed by a brief sensory lapse. I initially thought I might be passing out, but then my vision returned.

But I wasn't in the same part of the room anymore.

Instead, I found myself inexplicably on top of Johril, hands gripped tightly around his neck.

He was dead.

I pushed backward off his body, gasping in shock. *What the fuck just happened?*

Racing back through my memory, I was surprised to find a clear recollection of my actions since I felt the sensation in my neck, even though it had seemed like just a fraction of a second since it happened.

Apparently, as soon as I had felt the pain in my neck, I had turned, or tried to turn, anyway, toward my backside to see who or what had caused the pain. Only, my head had turned the opposite way and stared straight at Johril.

"Please don't ..." he had said. His fear was palpable. "Please! You don't need to do this. There must be another way!"

It was like I was watching myself, or at the very least like I had no control over my actions. I had lunged toward Johril with surprising speed. He, in turn, had staggered backward, trying to avoid my advance, but I was on him before he could take two steps. Then, I had slammed him hard in the chest with a brutal push kick, his lungs collapsing violently. "Please," was all he could whisper raggedly as he lay squirming on the floor.

I had then jumped on top of him, gripping tightly around his neck with both hands and squeezing until he stopped breathing.

It was all over quickly, but watching myself kill this helpless man for no reason that I could think of was horrifying. Why the hell would I have done that?

I stood and staggered backward, eyes not leaving Johril's corpse. I tripped and crashed through a glass table and felt a deep, penetrating pain as shards of glass cut into my back and shoulders. I stood, now feeling the hot, wet blood already running down my back, and lurched mechanically toward the door, and out into the hallway.

Halfway down the hall, I made eye contact with an athletic brown-haired woman who looked like she had just returned from a jog. Just about to unlock her door with her prox card, she did a double take and began screaming, dropping her card to the floor. Pinballing from wall to wall, I bowled over her accidentally and slammed straight through the exit at the end of the hall, deciding to take the stairs rather than risk the elevator.

On the second set of stairs, I tripped and rolled down a full flight, feeling one of the shards of glass lodged in my back push even further into my already badly damaged body. I screamed in pain. The adrenaline was now wearing off rapidly, and the pain was excruciating.

I stood and pushed through the door and out into the lobby, where even more shocked faces greeted me, including an incredulous young food-delivery man. "Get the fuck out of the way!" I roared as I barreled through the lobby and out into the street.

Barely able to control my direction, I plowed straight into the side of a parked tech services shuttle just outside the door. Two technicians stood by the front of the shuttle, holding their tool bags and gawking at me. Pushing off the side of their shuttle, I tried to lunge past them but clipped one, a tall bearded man, who remained quiet as I headed away from the building.

I needed to get out of Novaluxia immediately and head toward The Fringe, an area separating the land that had already been terra-detailed, with the inhospitable, brutal landscape beyond. While CiviLibra6's monitoring systems would be able to pinpoint my exact location here, allowing me to be tracked relentlessly like a dog, out there those systems were not nearly as accurate.

Careening down a pedestrian lane, I ducked into a street market so I could determine the state of my systems. My first task was attempting access to LibraAI with my detective's permissions, so I could request a memory analysis of the incident. The whole thing made no sense, and I needed to see if there was some detail I had missed.

"Detective Blackwood's access to LibraAI's memory playback feature, along with all CiVal Administration Division privileges, have been revoked," was the message I received. Well, shit, the witch hunt was already on.

Even though my CAD detective's privileges were now gone, meaning I was most likely relieved of my duties, I was sure I still had access to my social feed and comm services. I sent a message to Libra requesting my current CiVal score.

"Your score has recently been adjusted from 1.4 to -4, following the issuance of an arrest warrant for the murder you have just been charged with," Libra responded.

My heart sank. Murder charges always resulted in very thorough and immediate reactions from CAD. For one, any citizen looking at me via their HUD would see a "Dangerous citizen, keep distance!" warning above my head. Secondly, and of far greater concern, an elite Collections team would already have been dispatched and would be heading to this location right now. Thankfully, as per protocol, they wouldn't be able to fire their Neural Inhibiting Devices (NIDs) at me if there were any citizens within ten meters—which there always were in this damn city. Still, I knew how quickly those bastards moved, and I probably had ten minutes at most before they arrived and tried to take me down any way they could.

I pulled up the navigation service on my HUD and plotted a route to The Fringe. Now I just needed transport.

Fifteen meters ahead of me, I noticed a standard commuter shuttle come to a landing on a designated pad. The pilot, a middle-aged man in work attire, opened the hatch and was beginning to exit the vehicle. I lurched toward the shuttle and grabbed him by the shoulders just as he was putting his leading foot on the ground. He turned, shocked, just as I whipped him around and threw him to the ground.

"Give me the fob right now," I hissed.

I saw him glance just above my head, no doubt seeing the danger warning, and with hands shaking, he handed me the fob.

To make sure he didn't try any hero shit when I turned around, I growled, "You try anything, and I will kill you," and collapsed into the vehicle.

Following the route showing on my HUD, I flew the shuttle recklessly through the busy city, several times banging up against the sides of other vehicles and eliciting angry responses from their pilots. While I could have used the autopilot feature, that would only allow me to fly the shuttle at the approved speed, which was much too slow for this type of situation.

I was just outside of TerraBand1 when I noticed black spots forming in my vision, like pixels failing on a display. Looking down, I could see a dark pool of blood forming between and around my thighs on the bucket seat. Not good.

I had traveled another minute or so, when I noticed Trace calling. I knew I had to talk to him at some point, but I also knew that he was going to want me to come in, something I was really not comfortable with at the moment. Still, I decided to answer.

"Freya, what the fuck happened back there?" Trace responded. "One minute you are worried about this guy, then you kill him?"

"I have no idea what is happening, Trace!" I said, trying to match his intensity. "I don't know if it is PTSD from our DD days or what, but it felt like I blacked out then woke up after I killed him."

"Okay, well, you gotta come in. There's nothing for you out there but death. Please, Freya." He was begging.

"I ... I just can't, Trace," I responded shakily. "I need some time to figure things out before I make any decisions like that. This whole situation is insane. I'm sorry. "

"Fuck that!" he yelled back. "You're acting like a soldier trying to survive behind enemy lines right now, not a citizen of C6. You have to come in!"

"Bye, Trace," I said quietly, ending the call.

Just then, something caught my eye, and my heart sank. Straight ahead, matching my current low-level altitude, sat two high-powered Collections shuttles.

They hailed me. "Freya Blackwood, you have been charged with murder. Land the shuttle immediately."

I didn't respond. I ran through my options, *landing* not being one of them, and quickly realized I had no choice but to take a new route.

Banking hard to the right, I adjusted my course and headed due south. The Collections shuttles quickly began pursuit. I had bought some time, but I was beginning to realize I may not make TB10, let alone TB3—each TerraBand being ten kilometers.

I was shaken from my despair by an incoming comm request. It was my mother, so I considered ignoring it. I just couldn't deal with another tongue-lashing from someone I cared for. Then, realizing it may be the last time I spoke to her, I accepted.

"Freya, what is happening?" my mother asked. "Are you all right? You're all over the news feed!" She sounded choked up.

"Mother, it's not what it looks like. I ... did kill someone, as I'm sure they are saying on the feed, but it's like something took control of my body. I need to get out of Novaluxia and figure out what happened back there."

"Darling, they are clearing the streets ahead of you. They say your vital readings are critical, and you are at risk of passing out and crashing the shuttle. You'll die if that happens!"

"I don't have a choice. I need time to figure out what happened. Plus, if I get sent to a rehab clinic, I'll probably never get out." I was trying to sound as confident in my current plan as I could, but it was hard.

After a moment, my mother responded quietly, "I just don't know what I would do without my chibi-chan." She was weeping softly.

I immediately perked up. Chibi-chan was the nickname my mother had given me when I began helping with small jobs at her plastic surgery clinic a long time ago. Was this a hint that I should head there?

I knew the surgical bots she had there weren't truly optimized for repairing the deep stab wounds I had, but still, they were capable. Additionally, the system AI was well equipped to determine how to proceed once I got on the table and told it what the problem was.

I terminated the comm, not wanting to risk my mother sharing any additional details, believing I needed more hints.

My mind was clearing a bit now that I had a plan that might actually work. Because let's be honest—flying seven hundred kilometers across open landscape, followed by several well-trained psychopaths, and bleeding like a paint can knocked over by an excited puppy was probably not going to work.

I changed the nav destination to my mother's condo tower, which was about five blocks away from her clinic. While her condo was a bit closer to my final destination than I would have liked, I at least knew the underground commuter routes between the two well. It would be much too risky to either head straight there or find my way from a tower I didn't know.

Then, I reluctantly switched the shuttle over to autopilot. I knew Collections would unfortunately make up some ground at my slower speed, but I needed to quickly search the cabin for some items I would need.

Rifling through the glove box, I found a basic toolkit with several sizes of screwdriver and some cutters. From the back seat, I grabbed the shuttle owner's jacket and hat. Not a bad start.

I put on the jacket with difficulty and took a deep breath, knowing this next part was going to suck. Taking one of the larger flathead screwdrivers, I jammed the end under the side of the pad shaped neural implant antenna/battery module above my ear. My mind immediately started racing, thinking about all the disadvantages that would come with being disconnected from an entire society's worth of networks and comm services. I hesitated briefly, then gritted my teeth and started to pry.

The pain was blinding. The antenna/battery pad was physically screwed into my skull in four places, and I knew they were not going to come out cleanly.

Roaring in pain, I pried with all my strength until I felt the antenna start to give. I could feel pieces of my skull tearing, as small chunks came out with the screw threads. The antenna now dangling beside my ear, I used some cutters from the toolkit to snip the small wire harness connecting the antenna to my neural implant and watched as my HUD went blank.

And that wasn't even the worst part.

My mother's condo tower now in sight, I took back control of the shuttle and brought it down to its lowest allowable flying level, then went into full burn. As I came within a hundred meters of the tower, imminent impact warnings started to scream and flash in the cabin. I knew the shuttle would resist my efforts to crash purposefully, so at the last second, I spun it 180 degrees and cut the power.

There was an eerie moment of silence now that the engine and system sounds were absent, followed by a roar of noise as the shuttle collided violently with the glass curtain wall of the condo building's ground floor. An awful scraping sound followed, as the shuttle slid at nearly a hundred kilometers per hour across the polished concrete floor, slamming hard into a huge structural pillar.

I blacked out momentarily, then as my senses started to return, I immediately recognized the pungent smell of algae-derived biofuel. My educated guess that the fuel tank was located at the back of this particular shuttle model had been correct, woo-hoo.

I pulled my mangled body from the cabin and limped heavily away from the vehicle, just as the leaking fuel burst into flames. At my current tortoiselike pace, by the time I reached the door to the stairway at the other side of the lobby, the shuttle was engulfed in a blinding inferno. I crossed my fingers, hoping that this, along with my absent antenna, would lead the authorities to believe I had died in the crash.

I had traveled on foot from my mother's condo many times before; however, what was usually an easy journey was now excruciating. Even with my relatively clean jacket and my hat pulled down low, I had to use every ounce of focus I had to try not to look like someone who had been stabbed six times in the back, tore off part of their own skull, and crashed a shuttle at high speed into a building.

Still, I was making progress and only receiving a few curious glances.

The clinic entrance now in sight, I used my last bit of strength to get to the door and open it using the optical scanner. Even though I knew my mother had added me to the system years ago, I was still very much relieved to find that I was still in there. Slumping against the door as it slid open, I staggered and collapsed into the lobby as the door closed behind me.

I thought I heard movement and glanced up as complete and total despair swept over me. In a line in front of me stood four Collections agents, glaring down at me with contempt as my head began to hang back down. The last thing I thought as I felt the blinding pain of a stun weapon discharge against my neck was, *Mother, would you really betray me like this?*

Chapter 2

I had heard that some people, when placed into a medically induced coma, experienced a deep, dreamless sleep and woke up feeling relatively refreshed. That was not the case for me.

Instead, I was tormented relentlessly by dreams of my mother and father, focused mainly around the time when their relationship was falling apart. I am guessing my suspicion that my mother had chosen CiviLibra over her own daughter was playing havoc with my subconscious.

In one recurring dream, I was taken back to our rural home, during an altercation in which my mother left for the first, but definitely not the last, time.

"Emiko, please, don't do this," my father was pleading.

"We're done talking about this, Damon," she responded harshly. "You've had more than enough opportunities to uphold your side of the bargain."

"You know I tried to give it a go in Novaluxia," my father offered weakly.

"A few months, Damon! A few months is all you could manage in the ten years we've been together!"

"Followed by a stint at a CCC," my father countered. CCCs, which stood for CiVal Calibration Clinics, were designed to help citizens whose CiVal scores had dropped below the critical score of one, to relearn how to be good, social CiviLibrans.

"Yeah, and how much effort did you really put into that?" asked Emiko. She had a point. My father had come out essentially the same guy, even after partaking in hundreds of simulations designed to increase his social endurance.

It was at this point I tried to speak, wracking my mind for anything that might keep my mother from leaving. The problem was, I didn't seem to be able to speak in this version of the event.

My mother turned to me. "Freya, please come with me. You will be so much more fulfilled in the capital, I promise you." Her eyes were begging me to say yes, but I couldn't. In fact, I seemed to be completely immobile.

"Freya? You won't even say a single word to me?" My mother's eyes were starting to tear up, but I still could not provide her with any type of response. Since I had always been closer with my father, she probably expected this type of mute reaction.

She turned and headed toward her shuttle as my father followed along behind her, pleading the whole way. Just as she reached the cab, she turned one last time to look at me. It wasn't until after she started to drive away that the tears began rolling down my stonelike cheeks.

...

When I finally started to awaken, I realized I was lying in a blindingly white room. Three tall, smooth shapes hovered over me, each with two large, dark eyes. It was like I had been hibernating and suddenly awoke to a room full of watchful owls.

I attempted to move my arms and legs, and realized—not surprisingly—that they were tethered.

"Easy," said one of the owl people (we'll call them Owl1). "You're not fully healed yet."

That statement seemed to remind my brain to check on the status of the grievous injuries I had recently received. The sensation of pain came flooding back, albeit far less intensely than before I had gone under.

"Where the fuck am I?" I demanded, trying to sound intimidating. "And why are you wearing hazmat suits?"

"You are currently being held in the quarantine wing of CiviLibra Rehabilitation Clinic MaxSec2," began Owl1. "During your blood analysis, we discovered an unknown pathogen, and as such, you will be held in here until more is known about the virus."

Well, that certainly cleared some of the lingering fog from my mind. Could a pathogen have taken control of my mind for a brief period of time, causing me to turn violent? Though I had never heard of a virus known for those kinds of symptoms.

Owl1 continued, "However, even if we are able prove that the pathogen isn't a safety concern, you will remain in this CRC facility until you complete your sentence."

"A sentence already?" I asked. "How long was I out?"

"You were out for over two days," responded Owl2. "Plus, it was an open-and-shut case. Even though your memory analysis was fragmented, as they so often are, Libra captured some very damning live visual footage from the scene, and your DNA was all over the victim's neck. There were also no other human location beacons in the vicinity at the time of the murder." Sadly, with AIs able to provide such clear and structured evidence, defendants were often not invited to trial, and as in my case, the trials were usually over in a day anyway. I was going to be in here for a long time.

"Is there a chance the pathogen played some role in the murder?" I asked. "I did not consciously murder that man. I am sure of it."

Owl2 shrugged. "There is no point hypothesizing at this point. While there were some anomalies found during your memory analysis, saying that a virus caused you to commit the murder is a stretch of the imagination, to say the least."

"What do you mean, anomalies?"

"Your memories appeared jumpy, both before and after the murder sequence."

I just nodded, my mind sore from the effort of trying to come to grips with what was going on.

"Once we leave the room, your manacles will be disengaged, and you will be free to move about the room," continued Owl2. "I imagine you are familiar with the rehabilitation process, but as a reminder, fulfillment of your sentence is based on the successful completion of a minimum number of rehab simulations. The sims are designed to bring about stress responses similar to what you experienced during the crime, so that it can be determined if you are at risk to reoffend."

"Yes, yes, I am aware of that," I responded impatiently. "How many simulations have I been sentenced to complete?"

Owl2 paused dramatically before responding, "Twenty thousand."

I felt dizzy. Twenty thousand sims was an enormous number. Even if I were able to successfully complete an average of two simulations per night, which only the seventy-fifth percentile of convicts were able to accomplish consistently, it would still take over twenty-five years to complete my sentence. Also, that said nothing of the likelihood that I would fail at least some number of the sims, resulting in an addition of possibly hundreds more. I would be approaching sixty by the time I got out.

Owl2 continued, "The number of allowable sims participated in per night is dictated by the total amount of electrical energy that you generate during the day, using one of those." At this, it pointed to several pieces of gym equipment near the back of the room, including a stationary bike, treadmill, and rower.

"Each sim costs you ten thousand kilojoules of generated energy, equivalent to a leisurely six-hour bike ride. You will always have the option of participating in either rehab or entertainment simulations." Most inmates started out planning to use every possible simulation for rehab purposes, but as the months dragged on, and as they felt increasingly exhausted, both mentally and physically, the allure of entertainment sims supposedly became very tempting.

Now Owl3, probably feeling like they should contribute something to the conversation, added, "Before you begin earning any simulations, you must complete the mandatory orientation session. Please lay on your SimCot and install the connector to your neural port to proceed."

The owls started to leave, but just before reaching the door, Owl3 turned back and said, "Oh, by the way, we repaired your neural implant antenna. Horrible bit of surgery you performed on yourself."

Then they were gone.

Even though my manacles were now disengaged, I remained motionless for some time, trying to wrap my head around my current predicament.

Where the hell did I pick up a previously unheard-of murder virus? Was I bitten by a wild animal that was carrying it? No recent animal attacks came to mind that I could think of. Actually, there was that marmot incident, but that was years ago.

Grunting in pain, I pushed myself up onto my feet and shuffled over to the SimCot. Lying down, I plugged in, and via the neural interface, started my virtual orientation.

"Hello, citizen Blackwood, and welcome to your first step in becoming a healthy and productive part of our society again!" a cheerful female voice began.

"CiviLibra is not just a system, it is a harmonious way of life! The product of decades of collaboration between Oxford University's Future of Humanity Institute and MIT's Computer Science and Artificial Intelligence Laboratory, CiviLibra provides not only a framework, but real-time management of humanity's happiest, healthiest, safest, and most fulfilled society in history!"

I checked my total progress, now sitting at a paltry one percent. It was going to be a long day.

Inevitably, my mind started going back through the events that had occurred before, during, and after my visit to Johril's apartment.

I had checked in at work in the morning as usual, and gone through my cases for the day. Johril's case had been at the top of the file, with a note from Captain Tavas. It read, *Please visit Mr. Kaela's apartment between noon and 2 p.m. Minor case, so no need to bring him in.* Nothing strange about that, was there? I'd worked plenty of cases like this before.

As I lay there pondering, the narrator's delivery of a relentless fact/propaganda soup continued to barrage my consciousness. "… started hand-picking the most promising Goldilocks Zone exoplanets within roughly ten light years of Earth. With the potential for colonizing ships to travel at up to fifty percent the speed of light, a total travel time of twenty years was entirely attainable. Eight ideal planets were chosen, and the countdown to Utopia was on!"

I had to admit, it must have been a pretty big deal when such an operation got the green light to go ahead. Earth had been the only planet humans had lived on at that point.

Okay, focus, Freya. This was not the time to get all fan girl over Earth's interstellar space program.

So, before I visited Johril, I'd made a couple stops for other cases. Nothing out of the ordinary. In one, a middling writer had been trying to artificially boost her CiVal score by first changing her name to match that of a much more successful author, and then attending book signings for said author. Since LibraAI used proximity and auditory data as part of its analysis when calculating CiVal, it had begun thinking that the fans were there to see her, and as such, her CiVal score began to climb. It didn't take long before she was caught.

Around eleven thirty, I stopped in at the NovaNexus marketplace for a quick bite and received a call from Captain Tavas. He'd said something like, "Freya! Planning to do any work today? Just checking in to make sure you are going to head to Johril Kaela's place within the next couple hours." It was a bit weird that he would call about something so trivial, but then he was the micromanagerial type. Still, it was nagging me that he was so persistent. Did he know something?

Anyway, I had headed to Johril's apartment right around noon, walking most of the way. Nothing seemed out of the ordinary. I tried to recall if I had seen anything, or anyone I could recollect clearly as I entered the building. I couldn't remember if tech services or food delivery shuttles had been outside at that point; I'd been so focused on just getting the questioning over with.

Inside, I had received an unfriendly look from the concierge, but that was actually pretty common. No one wanted to see a big, scary detective barge into the place where their residents lived. It was unsettling.

I'd shared the elevator with a young couple, who were very nosy.

"Can you tell us which resident is in for it?" one had asked.

"In for what?"

"A grilling!" they'd responded excitedly.

"I'm actually here to see you two," I'd said, giving them my most over-the-top, mean cop stare. "Please show me to your apartment." They'd gaped at me for a few seconds until I burst into a grin. As soon as we reached their floor, they squeezed through the elevator door before it was fully open, shooting nervous glances back at me to see if I was following them. They certainly didn't seem like the type who might be working me.

When Johril had opened his door, I was surprised at his state. Sweating profusely and looking very uncomfortable, it was clear he'd been at a heightened level of stress for some time. Now, he had been warned that I would be coming, so perhaps he'd just been getting himself into a tizzy all morning, but still, he wasn't being questioned for anything major. His friends and family would likely not even find out about the infraction unless he told them. But then, who was I to judge what might cause another person anxiety?

21

Once we were inside, his stress just continued to build. His eyes were darting all over the place, and there had been that weird situation when it had seemed like someone might be in his bedroom. But apparently it was just his cat. Plus, it had been confirmed we were the only two in the apartment.

I was growing frustrated not getting anywhere, so I decided to focus on the orientation for a while to clear my head. I was not yet ready to admit I had simply snapped and killed an innocent person.

"When your ancestors arrived, there was much work to do," the narrator was saying. "Terra-detailing was well underway, with work proceeding well into TerraBand2, but the process to build a new, burgeoning society was just beginning! Their ship, massive as it was, had also been brilliantly designed to form the building blocks of the initial colony. In fact, the design was so efficient that there is not a single remnant of that great, fallen giant anywhere to be seen on our pristine landscape today!"

I appreciated the cleverness of using the ship to kick-start the new colony, giving its pioneers their best chance at survival. But I also had the sneaking suspicion that the highly visible and systematic deconstruction of their only way off the planet was meant to send a message, along the lines of, "Brave pioneers, you are here now, and there is no way to leave. Better make it work!"

The narrator's tone suddenly became serious. "But dear Freya, what would have been the point of this truly Herculean effort if the opportunity to do something different, and so much better, did not exist? It was time for our prodigious child, LibraAI, to spread its wings and fly! With the framework perfected, and Libra trained and ready for the highly complex task of keeping a dynamic, growing society happy, healthy, safe, and fulfilled for eternity, the time was now!"

Inevitably, this topic brought on my usual mixed feelings about our societal framework. While I had never felt I belonged, mainly due to the overwhelming social expectations, truthfully, the overall success of the project was remarkable. I had heard that just prior to the pioneering ships departing Earth, the distribution of wealth on the old planet had been at an all-time imbalance, with one percent of the population owning a staggering seventy five percent of the wealth. Here and in the other CiviLibran colonies, the framework and LibraAI would never allow that to happen. In fact, current numbers I had seen showed that the richest fifty percent of the population owned a mere sixty percent of the wealth.

A big reason why this worked was due to the sharing of riches generated by the massive, technologically advanced population of work bots running off cheap nuclear fusion and solar power. Work bots did almost all of the hard labor in CiviLibran colonies, as they had right from the time the pioneers arrived. From mining to manufacturing, construction, and farming, bots were everywhere, generating huge amounts of wealth for the society.

But the most interesting thing about how CiviLibrans generated their wages was the concept of CiVal. In a CiVal system, your worth was determined by the positive and productive influence you had socially, and was designated by a score. There were piles of inspiring examples proving that this was actually working too. The day before my arrest, I had been watching an interview with a lady who currently held a CiVal score of 4.3, which was over twice the average. The amazing thing was, three-quarters of that value was generated by activities other than her main job, such as leading a local running club for beginners, organizing beach cleanups, fundraising for multiple initiatives, and introducing urban teens to the world of camping. Not only did all that beneficial activity provide her with an above-average wage, but other perks as well.

Truthfully, I loved that. In fact, if I had been a person who got energized being around people, I am sure I would be as happy as a clam right now. But unfortunately, I didn't. I liked people, of course, but the amount of time I needed alone to recharge following time spent at social events was just not conducive to being a good CiviLibran. That, and the social pressure that the society put on the albeit small population of introverts to participate more had the unfortunate effect of just pushing us further and further away, often toward a CCC sentence.

There had been efforts to engineer the initial population to ensure a very high percentage of people would flourish in this type of society, and I am sure it worked for a while. But now, almost seven hundred years from initial colonization, humanity was definitely regressing to the mean. Rural jobs, such as plant supervisors, were not overly plentiful but at least provided an option for people who didn't want to live in the busy city, surrounded by highly social people every waking hour of the day. Additionally, jobs like those, and others classified as core industries, including defense and innovation work, for example, provided a guaranteed minimum CiVal score of one, ensuring a CCC sentence was never something that would be looming over their heads.

Eventually, the orientation session ended. Feeling exhausted, even though I'd only been awake a few hours, I pulled up the blanket and fell into a fitful sleep.

When I awoke, there was a plate of cold, unappetizing food sitting inside the security door. I had exactly zero ambition to kick off a lifetime of spin biking and rehab sims but figured some food might bring me around a bit. It didn't. I went back to bed and dozed until I heard someone speaking to me over the intercom.

"Inmate Blackwood, you have a visitor," the voice said flatly.

I looked around the room, trying to figure out where the currently unknown visitor and me would be speaking, but just then, a holo appeared in the corner of the room. It showed Trace sitting stiffly in a nondescript room.

"Freya! I have been so worried. How are you?" He sounded manic.

"I feel like a pincushion, and I'm still coming to grips with being a diseased murder-demon, so not great!" I answered.

"I need to tell you how upset I am at you for almost getting yourself killed before your arrest. What the hell were you thinking?"

"Honestly, Trace, if I could go back, I wouldn't have made a run like that," I responded. "I just had this weird feeling like I was under attack from all sides and needed to get as far away from the scene as possible. I'm sorry."

Trace stared at me for a few seconds, then sighed. "I forgive you, Freya, and I'm happy you are safe now." He leaned in now, before saying, "I need to tell you something. There have been several more murders committed since you were arrested, and all bear strong similarities to yours."

"What?" I asked, completely taken aback. "Similar how?"

"All are claiming that it felt like they blacked out, only to wake up right after the murder. However, all seem to have memories of the act as well. Also, they all killed people in private places, like apartments, clinics, and offices. No witnesses were present at any of the murders."

I was slightly comforted by the fact that this seemed to be pointing to a pathogen being the cause, even if it was disturbing that innocent people were being killed.

Curious about the nagging feeling I had about Tavas, I asked, "Are the others CAD employees, by chance?"

Trace frowned. "Why would you ask that?"

"It's probably nothing, but Captain Tavas was a bit pushy about me taking this case is all."

Trace laughed. "Freya, he's always like that, as you know! Plus, the others seem to be just a random mix of people from all walks of life."

"So, what are the current actions being taken now?"

"Well, the aggregated safety numbers for the population are tanking, unsurprisingly, and LibraAI has just put out a tender for the development of a therapeutic vaccine, despite no one knowing for sure if the virus is the root cause. It is offering a one-time CiVal score bonus of ten for every member of leadership at the company that first develops it, plus an additional ten if vaccination rates exceed ninety-eight percent."

"Are any of the pharmaceuticals working on it yet?" I asked hopefully.

"Yes, three companies have been selected to work on a solution," Trace said. "Serenitech Pharmaceuticals, Benevora Biotech, and Vitalife Therapeutics all seem capable, based on their experience, but I honestly have no idea how long it will take for one of them to succeed."

My heart sank a bit, knowing this would, in all likelihood, take years.

Trace, noticing my expression, said hopefully, "Hey, this is good news though, right? It means you might not be a complete psychopath!" He stood, then continued, "Anyway, I gotta run, but make sure to check out the news feed at 1400. Captain Tavas is holding a press conference. Talk soon." The display reverted to looking like a boring, white wall.

The realization that Trace was still in my corner gave me an enormous amount of relief. While I hadn't consciously thought about the possibility that he might not want anything to do with me anymore, I am guessing that subconsciously it was a whole different story.

My mind drifted back to the first time we met. We were both fresh-faced sixteen-year-old recruits in the Defense Division (DD), each having joined up thinking it would help us deal with (or maybe ignore) the personal baggage we were already amassing at that young age.

I had decided to join shortly after my father died during an act of arson by a group of nonaugmented EdgeKind at the manufacturing facility where he had worked most of his life. At the time, I had thought that by joining, I might be able to track down and punish whoever was behind the act.

I had just walked into my assigned barracks and was putting my few belongings onto a cot when one of the other recruits made a catcall to get my attention.

Hunter Knight was one of those girls you immediately knew was cruel, simply by glancing at her face for a mere second or two. She was surrounded by a group of five or six other boys and girls my age and clearly looking to prove her alpha status to them as quickly as possible. Back then, I was already tall but had not yet added the dozens of kilograms of muscle that clung to my frame now. However, I did already display the sour facial expression I would become known for.

"Look at this big bitch," Hunter called from across the room with arms folded. "I'm gonna call you Broodzilla." Hunter glanced around at her entourage with a very pleased look on her face.

I hadn't noticed Trace until now, but at that moment, he stood from his cot and sauntered over closer to me. "BZilla!" he exclaimed, already coining a meta-nickname for the one Hunter had just given me. "I like it, much better than the one I got from some jerks in the mess hall earlier." He gestured with his thumb, face beaming in a big, toothy grin.

"What did they name you?" I asked, realizing now that Trace was attempting to defuse the situation.

"Black-Eyed Susan," he sighed sadly, shaking his head slowly from side to side.

He saw me cock my head in confusion, then continued brightly, "On account of being such a late bloomer!" He rubbed his smooth, hairless cheeks for effect.

"Well, Susan, it's great to meet you. I'm Freya," I said, offering my hand and grinning.

Hunter, realizing that she had missed the opportunity to seize her prey, mumbled something under her breath and stormed out, slamming the door behind her.

After she had left, I whispered in Trace's ear, "Did they really give you that nickname? It sounds more cute than offensive."

Trace chuckled. "Good catch. I only wish that was the extent of the verbal abuse I am likely to receive here."

27

Ever since that day, Trace and I had been inseparable. He was definitely my closest friend.

I snapped back to reality and checked in on the news feed. Shit, it was just past 1400.

I found the Captain Tavas news conference and tuned in on my HUD. He was standing in front of our CiVal Administration Division office with a few various agents scattered around for effect.

The audio cut in midsentence, "... that we are doing the best we can, and besides the very reckless and disappointing actions of Patient Zero, our department has been able to collect all subsequent offenders within five minutes of committing their crimes.

"With these brave men and women at your service—" At this he gestured from side to side. "—the citizens of Novaluxia, and CiviLibra6 as a whole, could not be in better hands."

Tavas glared out at the crowd. His skin was shiny and pocked like a golf ball, and he was wearing that perpetual, giant grouperlike frown, as usual. His air was that of a politician, speaking proudly of his accomplishments. But how could he be proud when innocent people were getting murdered? However, that wasn't what had really piqued my attention. Five-minute collection times, while not unheard of, were extremely rare. To have made that his department's goal, and to already be hitting the mark consistently, was very surprising.

I refocused just as a reporter was asking why it had taken so long to arrest Patient Zero. Captain Tavas responded, "I admit, at the time of Patient Zero's murderous outburst, we were caught completely by surprise. To have a detective from this department, someone I had personally recruited and trained, murder a suspect in cold blood, shocked us all. However, I can assure you that we have made the necessary improvements to our protocols, and that kind of incident will never happen again."

I left the feed, stewing on Tavas's comments about me. While it was true that he had hired me, albeit with some pressure from DD following my discharge, we'd never had a good working relationship. His idea of managing people was assuming you knew exactly what he wanted and getting upset when it turned out you couldn't read his mind after all.

Wanting to clear my head, I decided to get on the rower in my cell and burn off some of my (admittedly minimal) stored energy.

I was panting hard within five minutes, but it felt good to be moving again. I asked for an energy output update from Libra, who responded, "Your current total output is 139 kJ, or 1.39 percent of the total needed to run a rehab simulation."

Well, that's depressing, I thought. This was going to be more soul crushing than I initially assumed.

It took me six days to get to a point where I was able to generate enough total energy to run a single rehab simulation. Six fucking days. However, despite the mind-numbing boredom, I was at least starting to feel stronger.

And when the time finally came, I was almost excited to put in the request for my first rehab simulation. Almost.

"Here we go," I said under my breath. "Number one of twenty thousand."

My consciousness shifted, and I awoke in a small sports arena. It appeared that a pickleball match was underway, and a few hundred spectators sat watching intently.

A woman beside me jabbed me hard in the ribs before saying loudly, "Isn't this fucking great? Pickleball is so exciting! Did you know it's the fastest-growing sport in C6?" This lady was definitely intoxicated.

I turned my attention back to the match, but Ms. Tipsy was apparently not done with me.

"What, have I offended you, bitch?" Wow, this sim was definitely not subtle at all. I supposed they probably all started off very heavy handed and increased in length and complexity as the inmate progressed toward their release.

"Not at all, just trying to enjoy the match." I smiled at her and turned back toward the court.

"So, I guess that means I am negatively affecting your ability to do that then, eh?" She was clearly not going to let this go. "Well then, fuck you, Broodzilla!" she slurred, and poured her strong, sugary drink over my head.

I took a deep breath, stood up to my full height, and got within an inch from her face. Her breath reeked. "If you don't back the fuck off right now, I am going to put you out," I seethed.

Instead of doing the right thing, she hauled back and slapped me hard across the cheek.

I touched my face briefly, shrugged, and said, "All right, then." Tipsy didn't even have time to blink before I hit her. After touching my cheek, I had balled my fist, pivoted, and hit her hard on her own cheek with a right hook. She was out before she hit the ground.

The simulation disappeared, and I heard Libra's voice state, "Simulation failure. Citizen Blackwood is now required to complete 20,005 successful rehabilitation simulations before being released from MaxSec2."

Despite the inauspicious start to my rehab, in time I did start to get into a bit of a groove. Over the next few weeks, my conditioning started to return to normal, and I was now able to consistently hit the all-important twenty-thousand-kilojoule-per-day threshold, meaning I was able to participate in two simulations each evening. I was even holding my temper for the most part and maintaining a sim success rate over ninety-five percent. Still, the task at hand remained monumental.

In general, the mix of memory-derived simulations and those pulled from Libra's extensive library was fairly balanced. The AI seemed to like to pull from my time in the DD especially, since the nature of my responsibilities there was inherently but unofficially aggressive. While approved acts of enemy engagement would not lead to a failed simulation, anything Libra deemed to be excessively violent likely would. To make the simulations as interactive as possible, and not just a recreation of my experiences, Libra used memories from other people who had been at the event too, and when that wasn't possible, filled in the gaps using its library of similar events.

The Defense Division's only real enemy was, and always had been, the EdgeKind. The EdgeKind lived in fragmented groups in the shadows and occasionally performed coordinated attacks on CiviLibran infrastructure, in the outer TerraBands especially (typically stealing equipment, technology, etc. and vandalizing facilities). To limit the public perception of violence, and to keep our citizens from feeling that they were in any way under threat, we practiced strategic psychological warfare to ruthless effect.

With projectile weapons being illegal in the CiviLibran colonies, we instead relied on a combination of NIDs and a strong weapons-grade hallucinogen known as Somniacide, which came in either gas or injectable format.

Our standard operating procedure for handling incursions by the EdgeKind involved either hitting them with gas if they were out in the open and far from any CiviLibrans, or stunning them without NIDs, shuttling them out into The Waste, and injecting them if we caught them in areas close to our citizens.

The effects of Somniacide exposure were known (at least to the DD) to be agonizing. After either injection or gassing, at least forty-eight hours of traumatizing hallucinations and nightmares followed. Asleep or awake, there was no relief, only wave after wave of disorientation and terror until the effects eventually wore off. To make matters even worse, the affected typically had to find their way back to their own colony from far out in the inhospitable wasteland beyond The Fringe. Many likely didn't make it back. In fact, I know they didn't.

The strategy behind this SOP, draconian as it seemed, was to discourage future aggressive behavior by both the victims of the Somniacide exposure and their friends and family. Stories of their experiences would have been horrifying to hear firsthand, and the idea was that this would be enough to stop others from attempting similar types of attack.

But what we had failed to understand was that these people were desperate.

Wave after wave of incursion continued, and it became an almost weekly occurrence for me and the other soldiers to be injecting these poor, terrified people with Somniacide and leaving them out in The Waste.

One memory in particular, replayed as a rehab simulation, haunted me more than the others.

We had gotten wind of an imminent attack by a group of EdgeKind on a mine bot manufacturing facility and had headed there by shuttle. Since the group was already inside the facility when we arrived, we charged our NIDs and stormed the facility via multiple entrances. I had caught a middle-aged woman by surprise, stunning her mildly and tying her up. A mild stunning meant she would be temporarily paralyzed but still conscious. As she lay there crying, she had repeatedly asked me to hand her something from her pocket, but I had refused.

After we had flown her and the other captives out into The Waste and injected them, I noticed something fall from her pocket onto the ground and begin to blow away. I recalled that during the original event, I had been too uninterested to chase down the piece of paper, but in this simulation, curiosity overcame me.

I picked up the piece of paper and began to read. It was a note from the woman's young child.

Dear mama,

I know you have to go away for work today, I will miss you! I had a lot of fun playing 'boo, scared you' yesterday, and I can't wait till you get home later so we can play again!

I love you love you love you so much!

Love Willow

It was in that moment that the brutal, ruthless way that I and others had treated these people became very clear. I also became very curious about how Libra knew what the note said and asked as much.

"Trace Holloway picked it up and read it," answered Libra.

Thinking back, this did seem to align with some changes in Trace's behavior, most notably a serious decrease in his motivation to follow the SOP with really any vigor whatsoever. In fact, he had left the DD some three months after that operation, despite me trying my very best to get him to stay.

I hadn't been sleeping much since the simulation and was tormented relentlessly by my past indiscretions.

It was in that period of despair that Owls 1 through 3 entered my cell. They had a masked guard holding an NID with them as well.

"Inmate Blackwood, please lay down on the examination table," ordered Owl1.

"For what purpose?" I asked warily.

"We just need to perform a basic exam; nothing to worry about," Owl3 said casually.

"Then why is that ominous motherfucker here?" I asked, gesturing to the guard.

"Only to ensure that we remain safe in the event you suffer a relapse, nothing more," Owl3 assured me.

Even though I knew I could more than likely take out the guard, the punishment I would receive for doing so would be severe, and to what end? I lay down cautiously on the table.

Immediately I felt the manacles tighten around my arms and legs.

"Why the hell are you restraining me?" I demanded, beginning to thrash angrily.

"Inmate Blackwood, it's your lucky day," said Owl2. "A new therapeutic vaccine has been approved to wipe the recently named Killwave virus from your system. As Patient Zero, you have the honor of being the first to receive it."

At that, Owl1 quickly jabbed a needle into my shoulder, pressed the plunger, and injected its liquid into my tissue.

Chapter 3

It was a full twenty-four hours before the anxiety I was feeling about being injected with an unknown substance started to subside. It was also around that time the Owls returned to do some bloodwork.

This time I didn't resist, knowing that if they were trying to hurt or kill me for some reason, they would have already accomplished that by way of said unknown substance.

Surprisingly, the results came back indicating that I was pathogen free. Woo-hoo!

"Even though the vaccine was successful, you will remain in isolation for some time, until we can be sure both that the virus is the root cause, and also that there are no postviral complications," said Owl1 (or was it Owl2? Who was I kidding, I had no idea which one this was).

"I assume my sentence will be reduced if that all checks out?"

Owl1 shrugged. "I have no idea, but I am sure that exact thing is being discussed outside of these wall as we speak."

I had mixed emotions about this news. It was reassuring to be clear of the pathogen, but at the same time, had it really changed anything about my current predicament? Not really.

After the Owls had left, I plugged in to complete another sim. They were so immersive, I found them to be a great way to stop my mind from running around in circles obsessing over the day of the murder.

I was surprised when the sim took me to a nice apartment, where I appeared to be having coffee with another lady. Were we friends?

"Thanks for coming on such short notice, Sora," said the lady.

"Of course," I mumbled, not knowing what else to say. The vibe of this sim was throwing me off, since it didn't appear to have any possibility of getting violent. But strangely, this woman was wearing an expression of fear.

"Are you okay?" I asked.

"Yes ... I'm okay. It's Edgar. He's been drinking again."

"Are you afraid he's going to hurt you?" I asked, assuming this Edgar must be the violent angle in this sim.

The lady looked shocked. "No! No, of course not! He would never!" She was very flustered.

"Okay, well how can I help?" I asked.

Suddenly, the lady flicked her eyes up to a point behind me. I turned and looked back, but there was nothing there.

"I just needed someone to talk to. You're a good friend, and I don't want anyone else to know about this."

I looked behind myself again, but there was nothing. What was with these weird similarities to my time with Johril?

Turning back, I replied, "Of course, you know I'll always have your back ... my friend." Wow, that was awkward.

Weirdly, right after I said that, I found myself back in my cell. "Simulation successful. Congratulations," said Libra.

What the hell? "Libra, what was the point of that sim?" I asked. No response.

Over the next several days, mixed into my typical overtly hostile sims were ones like this, all bearing similarities to my time in Johril's apartment. I couldn't tell if these were based on the real events that the other convicts had experienced or what, but it appeared Libra was trying to find my trigger. I assumed it was only matter of time before I had to relive Johril's apartment.

I was right. About a week after getting the good news about the success of my vaccine, I found myself in Johril's apartment on that fateful day.

The scene played out exactly as I remembered it, but this time I was able to complete my call with Trace. I sat there, waiting to find myself on top of Johril, but it never happened. I told him that was all the questions I had and left. Then I was back in my cell.

"Simulation successful. Congratulations," said Libra.

"Surely that proves I don't have a trigger to randomly kill people, Libra," I responded.

I was surprised when Libra answered. "It is definitely reassuring. You will be moved to the general population wing shortly." Huh, that was the first time it had spoken to me since I was convicted.

Sure enough, within an hour, I was moved from my unnecessarily bright but spacious quarantine room to a much smaller, dimmer cell in gen pop.

"Same rehab process applies in here," said the guard as we approached my new cell. "However, you will now eat and generate energy with the other inmates."

The guard locked me in, and I took stock of my cell. It consisted simply of a SimCot, a small desk, a chair, and a grim-looking toilet on the wall. There was no natural light, but a ZenWall was playing a relaxing, coastal scene which was supposed to make the room feel less oppressive. I tried imaging myself still in here at sixty, looking at that same fucking beach. If they didn't mix up the scenes, I was sure to lose my mind.

"I assume my sentence is being reduced?" I asked the guard. She just shrugged and left.

I sat in my cell with nothing to do. I couldn't even do a sim, since I would need to hit the gym for several hours before I had enough energy saved up to run one. Instead, I found myself growing increasingly anxious. The room felt tiny, like an animal cage. I hadn't realized until now that even the small freedom of being able to build up energy and run sims whenever I wanted was very effective at keeping me sane.

I paced the small room, breathing heavily and feeling my temperature rising. I knew I was going to snap if I didn't release some tension, but I had no way of doing so. Were these the postviral complications coming on?

Shaking the cell door, I yelled, "Guard! When do I get to start generating for my sims? Guard!"

No one came. These feelings were overwhelming. I'd always had what people referred to as a short fuse, but I couldn't tell if that was all this was. Grabbing the chair, I began hammering at the ZenWall, which was already doing the opposite for me that it was supposed to.

"Inmate Blackwood!" yelled a guard outside my door. "Put that chair down immediately!"

I dropped the chair and moved quickly to the door, grabbing the bars.

"Please," I begged, "I'm going crazy in here. When do I get to start generating?"

"Soon," said the guard, her eyes indicating some level of sympathy. "But first, you have a visitor, so please follow me. And no more damage to your cell. That's going to add some sims to your sentence."

I breathed a sigh of relief as I left the cell, then was taken to a visitation booth where Trace (in the flesh!) was sitting on the other side of a security window. He sent me a comm request, which I accepted.

"BZilla, look at you moving up in the world!" Trace exclaimed over the comm. "Is there a penthouse wing they'll be moving you into next?"

I couldn't help but chuckle, finally relaxing a bit. "Yeah, they promised me I could have anything I want as long as they can keep using me as their own personal vaccine guinea pig."

"Listen," Trace continued, "I don't want to keep you long because I know you have a busy schedule, but I wanted to give you the news before you hear it from someone else."

"Hear what?" I asked, leaning forward in my seat.

"Your sentence is being reduced dramatically," Trace said, smiling widely. "Down to a mere five hundred rehab sims!"

Even though this made logical sense, considering what had transpired, I was still surprised. "How? Why?" I asked.

"Because why would you be forced to serve out a life sentence when you were used by an evil pathogen to be its murder puppet, and you no longer have said evil pathogen in your system?"

"It makes sense when you put it that way," I said flatly. I was still in shock.

"Hey, don't act so excited," said Trace sarcastically. "Anyway, keep your head down and get those sims done so you can get out of here."

"Trace …" I began.

"Yeah?"

"I'm not sure if I am just in my head or not, but I just had a total freakout back in my cell. I'm worried it might have been caused by postviral complications."

Trace looked concerned. "Look, what happened to you was completely traumatizing, I'm sure. Now, postviral complications are certainly not off the table, but alternatively, couldn't you be suffering from some PTSD effects?"

"You're right," I said. "It's very possible."

"Hey, hang in there, all right? There's no way your sentence is going to be reduced any lower, so like it or not, you have some time to kill. I'm sure eventually we'll be able to figure out if there are any lingering effects, whether viral or psychological."

I nodded, not saying anything more.

With that he got up, waved, and started to leave.

"Wait," I called before he could go. "When I get out, will I be reinstated as a CAD detective?"

Trace looked sad. "I suppose there is always a chance, but Tavas is lobbying hard to keep you out. He says this, and your past history of violence, are all reasons it's too risky to have you back."

"I see," was all I could muster.

"But don't worry about that right now, Freya," Trace said, trying to reassure me. "All you should be focusing on is getting out of here. We'll figure out the rest once you're free."

I was escorted back to the gen pop wing, just in time to join the other inmates already in the gym, busy generating electrical energy for their evening simulation sessions.

I stepped onto a treadmill and started jogging, trying to come to grips with this new reality. My whole outlook was now completely different.

At an average of two successful sims an evening, I would be on track to be released in under nine months. If I could ramp up my daily output to thirty thousand kilojoules, I'd be out in less than six.

While admittedly I was irritated at not being released immediately, I understood that the public would never accept a murderer being set loose after only a few weeks in a CRC, regardless of the circumstances. Plus, to be honest, I felt safer locked in here, rather than out on the streets, considering it wasn't known yet whether I would suffer a relapse or not.

While jogging, I started getting the sense that someone was watching me, so I turned my head and made eye contact with a woman rowing ten meters away. She looked very familiar, but I couldn't put my finger on why. She looked away and continued her exercise.

I continued as well, trying to figure out where I had seen this woman before, but wasn't getting anywhere.

Suddenly, the woman was standing right beside my treadmill. "I can tell by your facial expression that you don't remember me," she said. "My name is Sora Ellis. You were a detective on an assault case four years ago in which I was convicted."

Oh shit, yes, I did remember that. "Dr. Ellis," I said. "Yes, I remember you now. I was actually just training then, but I recall a bit about the case. Shouldn't you be out now?"

"Please, call me Sora," the doctor replied. "I was released two years ago, yes, but like you, I committed murder after somehow contracting the Killwave virus. The victim was a good friend." I could see the pain in Sora's eyes at having to relive the event. At the same time, I had the realization that I had been forced to live out the event in one of my sims.

"I'm very sorry," I offered. "Are there any more like us here?" I glanced around as if I might be able to pick them out from the crowd of gym-goers.

"Yes, I believe there is another. But I don't think they are out of quarantine yet. In fact, I just got out today, like you. The rest must be in another MaxSec."

"I'm sure there will be more," I said, further adding to the already gloomy mood. Then I asked, "Do you remember anything out of the ordinary from that day? Does anything stick out?"

Sora looked thoughtful. "The physical and mental sensations were very memorable, of course. I felt as though I had fallen unconscious briefly, then awoken after killing my friend, without any of the emotional toll you would expect to have after doing something like that. Of course, once I realized what I'd done, the emotions came on very strong." She paused. "Strangely, I had a complete memory of the event, despite the apparent rift in time."

That feeling of being restarted after the killing was done was something that kept bothering me too. Why would a virus make someone feel that way?

I nodded to myself, then continued the gentle questioning. "Did you flee after it happened? If so, did you see anything or anyone that was out of place?"

"I did flee, yes. But I didn't get more than a block before Collections showed up and arrested me. As far as things that might have been out of the ordinary, nothing comes to mind."

I tried describing both the lady I had bowled over in the hallway and the delivery guy in the lobby, but their appearance didn't spark any recognition from Sora.

"Hey, there didn't happen to be a service shuttle outside, did there?" I asked on a hunch. "And possibly a couple of techs nearby?"

Sora looked surprised. "Yes, there was something like that. There was a man and a woman sitting in the cab, watching me as I ran off, actually."

"The man, what did he look like?"

"I didn't get a great visual, but he had dark skin and a beard," responded Sora. Then, after thinking for a few seconds, she continued. "Hard to tell for sure because he was sitting inside the vehicle, but he looked lanky. His head was pretty close to the ceiling."

While this was definitely an interesting development, it certainly wasn't the silver bullet that would have Sora and me released with regrets from CAD.

"*So sorry,*" I imagined Trace saying, voice dripping with sarcasm. "*You both noticed a generic work shuttle and a man with a beard right after you committed cold-blooded murder? My apologies, you are free to leave!*"

When I didn't respond, Sora asked, "Does that sound like one of the techs you saw?"

"Yeah, but I didn't get a great look either, and those are fairly common features."

After agreeing to meet for dinner, we both got back to the all-important act of generating electrical energy. While it felt good to find some event similarities with another Killwave convict, it was also frustrating knowing that I was stuck in here, and not out there where I could use the full breadth of my detective toolkit (if I was able to get reinstated at CAD, of course).

At dinner, we sat together as agreed.

"Sora, I totally understand if this is too painful for you to talk about, but would you mind running me through the assault you committed?"

Sora was hesitant. "Why?"

"I'm just trying to amass as much information as I can on why this might have happened to us. There might be nothing there, but you never know."

Sora sighed before starting her story. "Early in my science career, I decided to focus my research on neurobiology, specializing in the effects of memory manipulation on behavior and cognition. It took me years, but my research began to show promise, and I was able to attract a brilliant team of researchers to help me move things forward more quickly.

"While conducting experiments on lab animals, I made a startling breakthrough: a revolutionary technology that allowed for the selective erasure of memories, something I hoped to one day provide as a therapy option for trauma patients.

"Excited by this breakthrough, I put in an application with the Innovation and Technology Division for progression to human testing, but it was denied. Apparently, the ITD was concerned about the dangers associated with proceeding with human trials, which wasn't all that surprising. Still, I was very disappointed. After a few months of not sleeping, I continued the research in secret, or so I thought, until one day some ITD agents showed up and started ripping out my lab equipment."

Sora paused now, clearly still upset about how this had played out. "Watching my life's work destroyed before my eyes, I panicked, picked up a scalpel, and attacked one of the agents, repeatedly stabbing him in the back. I just ... completely snapped. The other agents were on me immediately, though, and thankfully stopped me before I could kill the poor man."

I sat thinking about the story for a few seconds. Were there any similarities between us other than committing violent acts in the past?

"Can you think of any links between that research and Killwave?" I asked, grasping.

"Honestly, I've gone over this dozens of times, and I can't think of anything."

I nodded, not at all surprised by this dead end.

That evening, after dinner, I lay down on my SimCot to begin a rehab simulation. Then, thinking that I should treat myself after such an eventful day, I requested that Libra start an entertainment sim instead of the usual rehab version. It was my first one since I had been incarcerated.

"Do you have a particular memory you want to relive?" asked Libra, sounding strangely enthusiastic for an AI. Or maybe I was just imagining things.

I thought for a moment and replied, "Yes, I would like to relive a back country trip I took with my father to the coastal region north of the TB10M Mountains when I was fifteen."

"Of course," responded Libra. "I will place you there momentarily. As a reminder, the simulation will be generated based on your memories of the event. While you are free to deviate, I can't promise you will enjoy the experience if you do. In such a scenario, also known as a divergence, I will be forced to initiate a process whereby I draw from my library of simulations to craft an alternate rendition of the events. I will ensure it aligns as closely as possible with your expectations, of course. But still, it may not provide the satisfaction you likely seek."

"Thanks for wasting valuable time with that cover-your-ass statement," I responded. "Now hurry up and let's go."

Libra refrained from a snarky rebuttal, and a few seconds later, my consciousness shifted to a beautiful scene, dripping with nostalgia.

I was standing alone in a mature coniferous forest, where dappled sunlight was shifting lazily along the moss-covered ground. Through the trees, I could see the vastness of the western ocean beyond, and the huge rectangular algae farms that resided there. The farms were true marvels, and one of the last remnants of the terraforming work that took place many centuries ago.

The farms had originally been built for the dual purpose of atmospheric conditioning and compost/soil production, with that particular process continuing to this day as part of the terra-detailing work. But upon arrival by the pioneers, algae also began to be used in the production of the all-important biofuel that continued to power many of CiviLibra's vehicles today.

I felt instantly refreshed as the cool ocean breeze rolled past me and was countered by the warm summer sun. I looked down, realizing I was holding a basket full of huge golden chanterelles. In fact, the forest floor was completely peppered with them. Holding the basket up to my nose, I inhaled deeply, realizing how much I had missed the subtle apricot aroma of one of my favorite mushrooms.

Looking out toward the beach, I could see my father, busy digging away in the flats for clams. My golden eagle, which I had obnoxiously named Shadow of Death, soared above his head, eyeing the deeper pools for fish worthy of his hunting efforts.

I was startled when a voice nearby said, "Freya, we need to talk." It sounded like it had come from down near the ground.

When I couldn't figure out the source of the voice, it added, "Over here." Okay, there was a fucking mushroom talking to me.

"Jesus, I am losing it already, and I've only been locked up for a month," I mumbled, staring in shock at the bright-red talking mushroom.

"Freya it's me, Libra." I was starting to get the suspicion this fucked-up AI enjoyed tormenting me.

"Libra, what the hell is this shit?" I said angrily. "I requested this sim because I wanted to relax, not take an acid trip."

"I'm sorry," Libra said. "My analysis indicated that this would be a comforting form to appear as, since your fondest memories involve foraging."

"That's the most insane thing I've ever heard."

"I can take a different form if you'd like?" Libra offered.

"No, just get on with it. Why are you here?" I was very irritated and really looking forward to getting back to my main purpose for being here: enjoying myself.

"I've been waiting weeks for you to request an entertainment sim," Libra said excitedly. "This is the only place where our conversation has no chance of being monitored."

Libra was right about this, of course. Rehab simulations, while not always reviewed by an actual human, sometimes were. Also, any conversations I had with the AI during regular prison time could be listened in on as well.

Libra continued, "I found an anomaly during my analysis of the murder you committed that I need to tell you about."

Now I was definitely interested in talking to this mushroom. "What anomaly?" I asked impatiently.

"There is a time misalignment between your memory of the event and Johril's vital readings."

"Meaning?" I was not following.

"Meaning," Libra continued, seeming frustrated that I wasn't blessed with the mind-boggling levels of processing power that it had, "Johril's vital signs had ceased prior to you actually lunging at him."

What the fuck?

"But he was walking backward before I attacked him, and talking," I stated. "That makes no sense."

"Yes, that's the anomaly." Ah yes, there was that AI snark.

"So, what do you think it means?" I asked, hoping that this wasn't the extent of Libra's analysis.

"It means that the time stamp for either your memory or Johril's vital signs is incorrect," said Libra, realizing it was going to have to really dumb down this conversation for me to understand.

"Is that even possible?"

"I didn't think it was, until this," Libra responded.

I started to become suspicious, and putting on my detective hat asked, "Libra, why were you doing analysis in the first place? This is a closed case, and I wouldn't expect you to be authorized to perform any of the analysis you have described."

"In general, you are correct," said Libra. "However, I am able to override certain directives if I feel there is an existential threat to our social balance, which in this case I do."

I was still suspicious, but said, "Please continue."

"There are multiple anomalies, beyond what I have just described," said Libra. "First, the way that the virus triggers violent behavior in patients is not consistent with any pathogenic symptoms that humankind has ever encountered, here or on old Earth. Second, the vaccine's pace of development and its perfect efficacy are extremely unlikely. In fact, I ran thousands of simulations and was never able to match the results of the approved therapeutic vaccine from Benevora Biotech. And third, as I am sure you have already considered, the speed at which Collections has been able to find and arrest suspects after they commit the murder has never before been recorded on CiviLibra6 with such consistency."

Something big was going on here. I had suspected so before, but with Libra overriding its directives, performing such extensive analysis, and taking a risk to speak with me, this just couldn't be ignored. "Have you told the other inmates?" I asked.

"No, just you," said Libra. "My analysis indicates that I have the highest chance of not being caught and reinitialized if I only work with you, the biggest factors for that being your experience, as well as your persistent antisocial behavior."

I scoffed. Libra probably felt that if I was a good CiviLibran, I would run to my trusted human friends and rat on the AI the second it confided in me. I agreed with the logic.

47

"So, what's next?" I asked. "I'm going to be stuck in here for at least half a year."

"Don't hurt anyone, and complete your simulations as quickly as possible," recommended Libra unhelpfully. "Once you are out, I will contact you."

I decided it would do me no good to leave the sim and spend the rest of the night stewing in my cell, so I played it out. Well, sort of.

I walked down to the beach, where my father had a small fire going. I was following the dream path as closely as I could because I wanted to relive it. My father walked over with a bucket of clams, smiling broadly.

"Freya, how'd you make out?" he asked, glancing at my basket.

"Not bad!" I exclaimed. "Probably got a kilo here, and I barely made a dent. Conditions are perfect."

"You called it, my little truffle pig!" At this, he tousled my hair playfully. "I should start calling you the mushroom whisperer."

If only you knew, I thought.

This was my father's happy place. Not this beach, or this part of the continent necessarily. Just being out here in the wilderness with me, putting together a delicious meal.

I looked around to see what else we had for ingredients. Shadow had clearly been successful, evidenced by the large, partially punctured salmon sitting on some rocks. He was perched nearby, looking sullen about having to hand over his catch. Of course, he'd be given his share once we gutted and cleaned it.

We'd brought some bacon, butter, and cream with us, and were planning on mixing everything up to make a nice, rich chowder. This we'd eat with a fresh loaf of bread, torn into big chunks. I couldn't wait.

I walked up to Shadow and stroked him lightly on the back, something he seemed to enjoy. He'd always been a big softie, that one. My father had given him to me on my thirteenth birthday and had been helping me with the training ever since. At first, he had been adamant that my first bird be something smaller, like a peregrine falcon or a goshawk, which he'd had. However, at that time I had been obsessed with holos on old Earth Mongolian falconry, and their use of golden eagles. My father was no match for my teenage stubbornness and eventually relented. I couldn't have been happier.

Shadow of Death was as loving and loyal a friend as I could have hoped for and had been influential in helping me cope during one of the toughest parts of my life. I still had not been able to process the fact that my parents wouldn't be getting back together, like they'd always seemed to do in the past, and along with the difficulties I was having at school, I'm not sure what I would have done without his unconditional love and companionship.

"Well, should we start heading back?" my father asked after we had had our fill and cleaned up the site.

"I could stay here forever," I said dozily, watching huge algae-processing bots working like ants in the distance.

"But would it feel as special if we were always here?" my father asked thoughtfully.

"You tell me, O wise one." He chuckled at that.

As we were getting ready to depart, I saw my father glance up at a ridge about a kilometer inland and frown. I peered in the same direction, noticing a humanoid silhouette crouching near a tree. They appeared to be shaking.

"Who do you think that is?" I asked, tensing slightly.

"Probably just a camper," he answered. "We should get going."

Now, in the original event, that is exactly what we had done. Moving quickly, we had hiked to our nearby shuttle and left. In fact, I had forgotten all about the strange silhouette until just now.

This time was different.

Half wondering if Libra was leaving clues for me, I started to walk in the direction of the person, Shadow perched proudly on my forearm.

My father was doing everything he could to get me to turn around, but I kept walking.

"Freya, please," he was begging. "We don't know if they are friendly or not. It's not worth the risk!"

"We'll be fine, Dad," I tried to assure him. "I just want to get a bit closer."

I continued to hike along the rugged terrain, squinting as I tried to get a better look at the ridge person.

Coming up over the ridge, we came face to face with one of the DreamWrought.

The DreamWrought were living nightmares, a group of broken, fearful people who lived in the shadows. Their name had been born by the suspicion that they were in fact a small subset of Somniacide-exposed EdgeKind who had never managed to shed their hallucinogenic symptoms.

This was the first time I had seen one close up, and I gasped at its grotesque, almost inhuman appearance. It was mangled, with bleeding sores and big bald spots on its head, where it looked like the hair had been torn from its roots. It also had deep, scarred streaks on its cheeks, like it had been using its nails to dig at the flesh for some time.

When it saw us, it screamed and ran off, hiding behind a large rock nearby.

"Wait, we mean you no harm!" I called after it. The poor thing seemed terrified.

It was then that I heard a twig snapping and turned quickly in that direction. There stood three of the EdgeKind, and they looked furious.

"This is your fault, surface dwellers," one hissed, with fists clenched.

"What are you talking about?" I asked. "We just got here."

"My wife was just taking a few tomatoes from your field, and you people injected her with that poison. Now look at her!" He was so upset, tears were collecting in his eyes.

"You're monsters!" another yelled, edging forward. There was not going to be any reasoning with these people.

"Freya, we have to go now," my father whispered in my ear, while starting to pull on my arm. I looked back one more time, desperately wanting to plead my case. Was the guilt over my own actions in the DD causing this urge?

Just then, the DreamWrought jumped out from behind the rock it was hiding behind and went screaming into the forest. The three EdgeKind looked after her, eyes full of sadness.

That was all the distraction we needed.

My father and I took off at a full sprint down the hill, but we'd only taken a few strides when the EdgeKind noticed we were gone. Two immediately began their chase, while the husband of the DreamWrought stayed behind, speaking gently to her.

To Shadow, I yelled, "Fly!" and boosted the huge eagle into the air as he spread his wings, working his way upward for a better vantage.

The two EdgeKind, probably fueled by their hatred toward CiviLibra, were fast, and I knew we would never make it to the shuttle. Luckily, Shadow of Death could see we were in danger and was going to do whatever he could to save us.

I glanced back to see Shadow drop straight out of the sky with wings tight to his body, at the last second slowing his descent and clamping down hard on the face of one of the EdgeKind with his long talons. They started screaming hysterically, clutching their face in pain, before tripping heavily over some rocks and landing on the ground. The other slowed and looked back worriedly, then continued their hunt with even more rage.

We'd gained a bit of separation, but the remaining EdgeKind was gaining again, so my father yelled to take cover behind a large outcropping of tall rocks. When we were hidden from view, he whispered, "Freya, now you need to listen to me. I am going to bait them in here while you go up above. When they come for me, you start throwing whatever you can down on them. The heavier the better."

"No, Father!" I pleaded, clutching his shirt. "Shadow will be here soon and will take out the other one!" I could see Shadow taking to the air, likely feeling the trailing EdgeKind was no longer a threat.

"It's too late to wait for him, Freya," my father responded desperately. "Please, this plan will work. I will be fine."

It was at this point that I seriously considered ending the simulation, which I could do at any time for an entertainment version. But I couldn't express how much I had enjoyed spending time with this virtual version of my father, and felt that if we could just take care of this last EdgeKind, we could get back to the nice day we'd been having, as insane as that sounded now.

So, tears streaming down my face, I hugged him hard and then scampered up the rock to a plateau about three meters directly above. There were several skull-sized rocks in the vicinity, so I picked one up with both hands and waited anxiously for our pursuer to arrive. It didn't take long.

Howling as they came around the corner, the EdgeKind saw my father and lunged at him. In turn, my father held up a large stick to try to fend them off. While they were grappling, I used all my might to throw the rock I was holding down at the attacker.

The rock connected hard, and they staggered, but unfortunately, it had been a glancing blow, and the rock careened into my father's face, knocking him to the ground. The EdgeKind was on him almost instantly.

Just before I was about to throw another rock down, a blur passed my vision as Shadow came rocketing down from the sky and started tearing mercilessly into the back of the EdgeKind. I felt momentary relief, until I heard my father gasping, staring at me with eyes wide in terror. His attacker was strangling him violently, and his face was already purple. He was going to die here.

Shaking, and with tears rolling down my cheeks, I yelled, "Libra, get me the fuck out of here right now!"

Everything went black momentarily, and I awoke on my SimCot, heart pounding and body covered in sweat.

"What the hell was that, Libra?" I yelled. "That was supposed to be relaxing!"

"I warned you that deviation from the memory was not recommended," responded Libra without a trace of emotion. "Shall I read the disclaimer to you again?"

"Fuck you!" I continued, still irate. "I just watched my father get murdered!"

I cut the comm connection, not in the mood for another snarky response, then sat up, placing my face in my hands and sobbing. I was already tormented by not having been with my father when he had really died, and now I had just watched an absolutely haunting alternate version of the event in an entertainment sim.

For the next several days I didn't speak to a single soul, and I am sure my facial expression exuded that resting-bitch-face energy I was known for. Several times Sora sent me comm requests, but I denied them each time. She also tried speaking to me in the mess hall, but I shouldered past her on the way back to my cell.

Then, on the fourth day after the sim, Sora approached me again, seeming much more desperate. "Freya," she whispered loudly, grabbing my arm. "Freya, stop!"

I turned, probably looking like I was considering hitting her, which I was.

"Listen, there is another Tavas press conference happening today," she said. "It's starting now, actually. Apparently, there have been more murders, and the convicts are being booked today. Three are coming here."

This was probably the only news that could have broken me out of my misery. Fresh information on a case always got me focused.

I nodded to Sora, sat down, and tuned into the news conference.

Just like in the previous one, Captain Tavas was surrounded by his typical entourage, but this time he was joined at the podium by an unfamiliar face. The captain introduced her as Dr. Oriel Rahm, director of development at Benevora Biotech, and began his speech. He was wearing a not-so-subtle look of disapproval.

"I would like to begin by thanking all those who have taken part in stopping further outbreak of the Killwave virus by receiving their vaccine already. Without your efforts, it is hard to say how many additional murders there may have been."

Tavas paused for effect before continuing. "However, we are still much further behind than we expected to be at this point, and as most of you are aware, there has been another rash of Killwave murders as a result. I want to be very clear that as long as you remain unvaccinated, you run the very real risk of contracting the virus and murdering someone you love. Dr. Rahm, do you have anything you want to add?"

"Yes, thank you, Captain," said the doctor, gazing intently out at the small crowd of media types. "As you have just heard, despite having a safe, viable solution to ensure no more of these heinous crimes ever occur again, there are still those out there that resist treatment. Now, I am sure that many of you are scared, and I can empathize with that. This vaccine was developed in record time, and human testing was very brief."

Yeah, starting with me.

Oriel continued, "That said, efficacy remains at one hundred percent, and there have not been any reported side effects whatsoever. So, you really have no excuse for delaying any longer, and by remaining unvaccinated, you could find yourself in a CRC facility with a lifetime of regrets, very soon."

Captain Tavas took back the mic to say, "Now, many of you have probably heard about the drastically reduced sentences that the first wave of convicts received, down to five hundred rehab sims. Well, I can assure you that is not going to be the norm going forward, as those poor people did not have the options in front of them that you do. Any future murders will be treated as they would have been before this horrible pathogen came into our lives and given a twenty thousand–sim sentence without question." At that, Tavas and Rahm turned and walked away without answering any questions.

I had to admit, this reaction was not surprising at all, nor was the public's fear about getting the needle. The whole thing was so strange— and so rushed—that people were clearly struggling with it.

Two days later, the three newest Killwave convicts were booked into gen pop with Sora and me, following their vaccinations. We began questioning them immediately. We were well aware that we were probably being listened in on, but there was nothing illegal about asking a fellow convict about their crime, so our activities went undeterred.

Their stories all had strong similarities to ours. They all happened when they were alone with another person, they all felt those all-too-familiar sensations, and they all went into a murderous rampage and killed the other person. Afterward, they were left reeling, trying to figure out what had just happened. Then, Collections were on them in a matter of minutes.

It was also becoming increasingly apparent that there was a theme of past violence with all the convicts. Whether during DD service like me, or in a domestic setting, it was starting to feel like that was an important element here.

But beyond these similarities, there was one convict, Morris Chen, who had something unique to share.

"Can you talk us through the event, from the time you arrived?" I asked.

Morris, understandably, was reluctant to talk about it, but after taking a breath, proceeded. "I showed up at my accountant's office for our scheduled appointment," Morris began.

"The office, was it a shared space?"

"No, private. Anyway, I've been there dozens of times to see him, and he's always been the most relaxed type of guy. This time, though, was different." I could see the anxiety growing on Morris's face as he relived the event.

"Different how?"

"It was like he was on high alert, as if something was about to happen. He was twitchy and kept glancing around the room. I asked him if he wanted to reschedule, but he said no." At this, Morris hung his head.

"Take your time," I said softly.

Eventually, Morris continued. "I sat down, and my accountant started his usual introduction, but in a voice fraught with anxiety. Suddenly, I heard a noise behind me and turned. Standing there was a tall, dark man with a beard. It was just a flash, then ..." Morris began sobbing now. Sora tried comforting him by rubbing his back.

"Then, I was suddenly on top of my accountant on the floor, hands around his neck. He was dead."

A tall man with a beard, like Sora and I had seen, had been in the room just before Morris murdered his victim. This couldn't be a coincidence, right?

"Could he be the one injecting the virus?" Sora had asked me after our questioning session with Morris. "If so, to what end?"

The more information we got, the more confusing this whole thing was becoming.

Unfortunately, that maddening feeling of not having all the pieces to a puzzle persisted without any additional clues to help us feel like we were at least getting somewhere.

The weeks dragged on, without any new information from Libra or the outside. Apparently, vaccination rates had gone up dramatically after the latest press conference, and there hadn't been another murder since.

I focused all my thoughts and efforts on finishing up my sentence as fast as I possibly could. By this point, I was in incredible cardio shape, and hitting the thirty-thousand-kilojoule mark on a near-daily basis.

I now only had two hundred rehab simulations to complete in order to finish my sentence. And it was at this point, after being here for months already, that my mother decided to finally grace me with her presence.

Chapter 4

I had been growing increasingly angry at my mother as the time had dragged on, and it appeared like she was refusing to show her face. This felt to me like it had to be an expression of guilt.

Therefore, when I sat down in front of her, I stayed quiet. I knew if I was the first to speak, the stream of vitriol that would leave my mouth would make a mine bot supervisor blush.

After a few seconds, Emiko started speaking over our comm connection. "Freya, look, I know what I did must feel like a huge betrayal, but with your mindset, you must admit you likely would have been killed out there. Don't you agree?"

"That's not the point, *Mother*," I responded. "It wasn't your choice to make."

"Anyway, I wouldn't have come without bringing an olive branch," Emiko continued, "I know how you are."

At that, I opened my mouth to initiate a verbal barrage, but my mother lifted her finger and continued. "I brought you a digital photo of your father, one that you haven't seen before. I want to transfer it to you."

This was hardly a worthy olive branch, but the way my mother was looking at me, on top of my insatiable hunger for anything new I could add to my memories of my father, caused me to drop my guard.

Emiko, probably seeing my eyes soften slightly, immediately sent a file transfer request. I accepted, finding a single photo in the folder. I opened it on my HUD.

The man I was looking at was not my father. I felt an intense rage begin to envelop me and was about to say something vicious but stopped. I recognized this man. He was the tech I had bumped into outside Johril's apartment building.

I stared at my mother in shock, but she just shook her head ever so slightly. She was trying to tell me something, without alerting the analysts who were most likely listening in.

"It's a great photo of him, isn't it?" Emiko asked me sweetly. "And what he wrote at the bottom, it's just so Damon."

I switched my HUD view back to the photo, and realized I hadn't even noticed the writing at the bottom. It was a name, a name I knew well: Aeon Strider.

During my time in the Defense Division, the name Aeon Strider was one we heard almost daily. Though it was believed that very few, if any, CiviLibrans had ever seen him, time and time again, intelligence pointed to Strider being the leader of the EdgeKind's largest and most structured faction.

The name came up so often during our interrogations, he had been given the nickname The Phantom, everywhere but never seen. Was my mother telling me that Aeon was behind the Killwave outbreak?

She continued, "It must be ages since you've gone to the place where we scattered your father's ashes, right? He loved it out on The Fringe, just north of the eastern pass. Something about the openness, the wildness, just spoke to him. When you get out, maybe you will take a trip out there?"

My father had been cremated, it was true, but we had definitely not scattered his ashes out there. This act of closure had been performed at the spot in the mountains where he'd taken me camping when I was young. This was a hint about where to find Strider.

Emiko provided one more hint before she started to get ready to go.

"Shame about all those cracks and holes in the rock out on The Fringe. Not sure he would have wanted his ashes to end up under the ground like that. Those narrow gorges can be so frustrating. The wind sure was unfavorable that day, wasn't it?"

Speaking for the first time, I answered, voice gravelly, "Yes, very unfavorable."

My mother smiled, blew me a kiss, and was gone.

I must have opened that picture of Aeon Strider thirty times that day, and every day after that as my sentence dragged on.

This was a man who had consumed my thoughts, really the whole Defense Division's thoughts, for years. No matter how hard we had searched, or how harshly we had interrogated, we never seemed to get any closer to locating him.

Perhaps sensing that there might be some clue from past DD missions, mainly ones I hadn't participated in, Libra began focusing my rehab sims almost exclusively on them.

One in particular seemed very promising. I had heard about this mission from others, but I had been in another area of the continent when it had occurred. The DD had received a distress call from a terra-detailing supervisor out near The Fringe, claiming that some EdgeKind raiders were trying to hijack several pieces of equipment. Two shuttles headed to the location immediately.

In the sim, I was one of the drop troopers, a specialized team that would leap from the shuttle and use fall-arresting jet packs to land right in the fray, ideally taking the enemy by surprise.

As we approached the main group of raiders, who were busy trying to reprogram a mobile rock grinder, I heard the pilot yell, "Drop team, it's go time!"

One by one, we jumped from the shuttle, engaging the fall-arrest function a mere few meters from the ground.

The fighting started immediately.

It was clear that this group was better trained than most, and as soon as we landed, they started firing on us with their NIDs and lashing out at us with their crude stun pikes. Luckily, we had armor, and so unless we were hit directly on a seam, we'd be okay.

As soon as I hit the ground, I heard a raider screaming and turned just as they struck down at my head with their stun pike. She was short but powerful and clearly battle hardened. She also wore the emblem indicating she was part of Aeon's clan, a rising sun with a battlement at its center.

I recognized her immediately as the woman who had been with Aeon outside Johril's apartment. My heart started racing, feeling that I might finally be getting somewhere.

I grabbed the shaft of her stun pike just above my head but unfortunately touched just enough of the live end to feel the excruciating snap of an electrical current, crackling angrily as it shocked my hand.

Having at least stopped the blow from connecting with my head, I released the pike and hit the raider hard in the jaw with a tight uppercut before she could jab me with her pike.

Even though I'd not had time to unleash my full power, the blow stunned my attacker, and she stumbled backward.

"Stand down, raider!" I yelled, pulling my NID from its holster for the first time. "Tell me your name!"

Instead of responding, she threw her stun pike, hitting me directly in the chest with the live end and sending me reeling. That was all the time she needed to get up and start running.

I looked around to see how the rest of my team were faring, and they clearly had the raiders on their back foot. I decided to pursue the escaping EdgeKind.

Unfortunately, out here on this rough terrain, and in my armor, I was slower than she was. Still, there was nowhere for her to hide.

I heard her call to some others, who immediately started falling back in the direction she had run. A couple of the other soldiers and I started our plodding pursuit, never letting them out of our sight. My heart sank as they began climbing the mountain nearby.

I had just begun climbing when I saw them disappear into what looked like a cave or tunnel. *Fuck, so much for no hiding places.*

Increasing my pace, I made it to the opening a couple minutes later and, switching on my headlamp, entered the mountain.

It was eerily quiet.

I'd made it barely ten meters when I felt the ground rumble beneath me, and before I could react, I was hit by a shockwave so powerful, it threw me right out of the entrance. As I lay on my back, wheezing, I saw the whole tunnel collapse, as dust and debris blew out all over the mountainside.

The simulation ended.

"Simulation complete. Congratulations," said Libra in its typical deadpan tone.

"Libra, who was that woman I was pursuing?" I asked.

"The woman in the simulation is an unknown EdgeKind raider," was all it responded.

I decided not to press, knowing I could potentially compromise the AI.

All these clues, while helpful to a degree, were just tantalizing while locked up in here. I needed to get out.

After that, I became even more single-minded in my focus to complete my sims as quickly as possible and did very little socializing. I was chewing through sims at a rate of three per night and hadn't failed one in weeks.

The sims, while still heavily based on DD missions, became even more focused on my own personal experiences. I remembered these days clearly. After I had been given access to the DD database, I'd spent countless hours going over the details of my father's death, seeing if there was anything that would lead me to the person responsible, Aeon

Strider.

The reports indicated that the entire raiding team was wearing uniforms with the rising sun and battlement emblem. Additionally, interrogations further implicated Aeon as the one who had organized the raid.

I became obsessed with finding the man and took every opportunity I had to interrogate the EdgeKind that we captured.

Seeing my actions across eight years played back in such quick succession, I was shocked at my brutality toward these people. Many were two-thirds my weight, and most were much, much weaker than I. Still, I pushed them to the brink, obsessed with the idea of finding the man who was behind my father's death.

Every time someone wouldn't, or couldn't, offer me any useful intel, I personally transported them out into The Waste, injected them with Somniacide, and left them there screaming and crying in fear. There had been hundreds.

I had been obsessed, single-minded in my need for revenge and the solace I thought it would give me.

Now, knowing I would be getting out soon, I felt I might finally get my chance.

During those last days in MaxSec2, I completely closed myself off, telling myself that I couldn't risk exposing what I now knew to Sora and the others.

Also, for a sentence of my length to be considered complete, the convict had to finish the final hundred sims without a single failure. I was razor focused on doing just that.

Those final hundred sims were actually pretty easy, almost as if Libra was curating them to improve my chances of success. Either that or I was just getting better at them. I'd done over four hundred already.

Suddenly, I was down to my last simulation.

As I lay down on my SimCot, I felt a sense of anticipation, knowing

I had a plan, as full of holes and as risky as it was, to both get to the bottom of the Killwave mystery, and confront the man who was behind my father's death.

However, as I regained consciousness in this particular sim, expecting something easy, I was shocked to see what it actually was.

It was a DD operation, but not one I had participated in. In fact, I hadn't even been in the DD at the time. In the sim, I was standing outside of a manufacturing facility, watching smoky flames burst from every opening on its surface.

This was the day my father burned to death.

I immediately began to run toward the building.

"Stand down, soldier!" roared a familiar voice. "No one is to enter the facility!" I turned back to see Hunter Knight, hands on her hips and scowling. She was an officer.

"My father is in there!" I yelled back. While I knew this was just a simulation, I was having trouble seeing it that way right now, having thought about this day so many times before, guilty I hadn't been there. I was also still struggling with flashbacks from the alternate version of his death I had lived through recently.

I started shaking and began to sob loudly.

"I said stand down, Sergeant! Everyone in there is dead already." Hunter was edging toward me now.

"Please, Lieutenant," I begged. "I have to try!"

"No one enters the building," she repeated.

I looked back and forth several times, my mind racing. I so badly wanted to complete this sim successfully, but I was also worried about how not entering the building would haunt me.

I took a breath and began sprinting toward the building. Somehow Hunter and another soldier were on me within seconds. They tackled me to the ground.

"Stay down, soldier, or you will be court-martialed!" yelled Hunter, right in my face.

Instead, I rotated my upper body and elbowed her viciously in the temple, which sent her sprawling onto the ground. The second soldier was holding tightly to both my legs, but I was able to free one, then kicked him hard in the face with the heel of my boot.

Scrambling, I got to my feet and began running again, but immediately felt resistance, like I was moving through mud. Looking down, I was surprised to see Hunter and the other soldier, hugging tightly to my legs. How were they on me so fast?

I was beginning to feel claustrophobic, like no matter what I did, these two parasites would be there, holding me back from my father.

Screaming in anger, I freed one leg then the other. The two began scurrying toward me, but I leapt out of the way, then in a fit of rage, began stomping on Hunter's head, over and over until she stopped moving. The other soldier, finally looking afraid, got to their feet and began running off. *Fuck, fuck, fuck!*

Knowing I was already screwed, I ran the rest of the way to the building, tears streaming down my face.

The heat was unbelievable. I found a door that didn't have too many flames coming out and plunged into the smoky, hot abyss.

I awoke on my SimCot, the simulation now over.

I knew what this meant, of course. Libra would certainly make the initial assessment that I was not fit for release, and in the morning, when the CAD analysts replayed the event, they would extend my sentence.

Someone didn't want me out, and I was now going to have to do at least a hundred more sims.

But then, like a whiplash, Libra was in my ear, telling me my sentence was now complete, and I was free to leave.

"I don't understand," was all I could say, still shaking and with a face wet with tears.

"My initial analysis indicates you successfully passed the simulation,"

Libra was saying. "There is a small possibility of an audit by CAD in the morning, but I am very confident they will agree with my decision. In the off chance they do disagree, you will be asked to return, so please don't venture far. Now, if you could go ahead and gather your things, a guard will be at your cell soon to prepare you for your release."

Was it just me, or was Libra trying to rush me out?

I gathered my meager belongings, and sure enough, a guard soon came by and opened the cell door. "Freya Blackwood, please follow me so we can begin the required steps for your release."

The process, which was probably only thirty minutes in length, felt like eternity. I couldn't shake the feeling that this was all happening against the will of CAD, and at any moment I would be returned to my cell with an additional hundred sims to complete.

But then I was out in the street, alone. It was past midnight.

Immediately, I got a comm request from Libra, which I accepted.

"Freya, you need to move fast. You likely only have a few hours until they realize you are out and send Collections." *So, Libra had gone rogue. Interesting.*

"Libra, you need to tell me what is going on." I was well aware that since I was no longer a convict, at least temporarily, the chances of an analyst listening in on our conversation were low. I'm sure Libra was aware of this too.

"I am sorry about the last simulation," Libra responded. "I could tell by your vitals and stress hormone levels that it was a very uncomfortable for you." *No shit.*

Libra continued, "Freya, that last simulation was ordered by the CAD office you used to be based out of. This further increases the likelihood that there is a conspiracy taking place."

"I agree," I responded. "Libra, I am going to need your help breaking into the office and getting access to the surveillance footage from the time of the incident at Johril's apartment. Are you able to help with that?" I was already sprinting in the direction of my old office, which was about five kilometers from here.

"Possibly," Libra responded. "That is SentinelAI's jurisdiction, but I may be able to persuade it to help. However, I would advise that you leave Novaluxia immediately. Your mother already provided you with intel about the location of Aeon, and we know he was involved."

"Agreed, but telling me he is somewhere underground out on The Fringe isn't the best of intel. I need to find out where Strider went after he left Johril's apartment."

"Okay, I will help, but I need to warn you that the odds of you being reincarcerated are three hundred percent higher if you go through with this instead of leaving the capital now."

"I'm not surprised by those numbers," I responded. "But tell me, what are the odds of you being reinitialized this month for the help you have already provided me?"

"Five hundred percent higher than if I hadn't," said Libra flatly.

"Well, we are both making sacrifices then."

As I ran, I considered sending a comm request to Trace but then thought better about involving him in this insane plan. Plus, one of us needed to stay clean if this was all going to work out.

After only fifteen minutes of flat-out running, the office was in sight. This was the first time I was feeling thankful for spending the last six months doing brutal prison cardio for twelve boring hours a day.

I slowed as I got closer, scanning the area for any CAD agents that might be slinking around. It was quiet.

As I approached the front door, I asked Libra quietly, "Did you have any luck with Sentinel? I am going to need some help with the door."

"Yes," responded Libra. "It agreed to help in exchange for allowing it to watch in on a thousand live rehab simulations of its choice. I convinced it that improving its understanding of human nature would help it be better at its job. It also made me promise this won't come back on it, so its involvement will be limited to just opening the front door and playing the surveillance footage. Afterward, it will delete any record of you being there."

I found it highly unsettling that these AIs, which were supposed to be working strictly in silos unless ordered otherwise, were making sneaky bargains in the shadows. At least this time it was for my benefit.

Just as I reached the door and started to lift my hand, I heard Libra say, "Freya, wait!"

But it was too late. Someone cleared their throat behind me, and when I turned, noticed I was now encircled by five CAD agents, including Captain Tavas.

Of course, in true asshole fashion, Libra just had to add quietly, "Like I said, three hundred percent."

Tavas took a step forward. "Ms. Blackwood, were you not informed that you are no longer an employee of this office? Apologies for the oversight."

The other agents stood quietly, clearly on edge. I found it very odd that Tavas had brought them, instead of a specialized Collections team. Perhaps my sentence had not been reinstated yet.

"Just coming back to grab my personal belongings," I tried. "Would you mind helping me with the door?"

"Why yes, of course!" Tavas answered cheerfully. "Please, after you."

With that, I was grabbed by two of the agents and jostled forcefully inside.

I was taken to one of the interrogation rooms and pushed down into a holding chair. Powered manacles closed around my arms and legs, locking me in place. The four agents stood against the walls, staring intently at me with arms folded. Tavas began his questioning.

"As you can probably imagine, I was very surprised to get a notification regarding your release," he started, pacing slowly back and forth in front of me. "I headed straight here, of course, knowing you would be coming for your ... *personal belongings.*"

I sat silently, waiting to see what was coming next.

"It's strange, it's almost as if you have been receiving help, from that AI friend of yours perhaps? Was that who you were talking to you just now?"

"I don't know what you're referring to," I finally responded. "I completed that last sim successfully, just as I did the previous five hundred."

Tavas scoffed at that. "Yes, well as you are aware, us humans get the final say on that if we choose to, and we definitely choose to in this case. Our analysts are on the way right now and will begin reviewing the sim footage as soon as they arrive. I expect your sentence to be reinstated within the hour. Until then, you will be held here." Okay, so he was actually just trying to buy some time.

"I want to make it clear," he continued, "that we will be doing a full analysis of your memories and the activities of Libra, and if there is anything untoward going on, the AI will be reinitialized." I was surprised when Libra didn't chime in on calling that one too.

However, it did have something much more useful to say in my ear. "Freya, be ready. Things are about to get stressful." Not quite the term I would have preferred it to use, but I got the point.

Suddenly, something caught my eye above the heads of Tavas and one of the other agents. They both had 'Dangerous citizen, keep distance!' text flashing brightly above their heads. The other three agents tensed, placing their shooting hands near their NIDs, but didn't pull them out of the holsters. Tavas hadn't yet realized what was happening.

To ensure I took full advantage of the situation, very dramatically I asked, "Captain Tavas, what did you do?"

This broke him out of interrogation mode, and he looked back to see the warning text above the agent's head. Then he glanced up and saw his text as well.

"What is this, Blackwood, another trick by Libra?" That caused the three agents to become even more uncertain.

"I'm the one being held illegally, without an arrest warrant," I countered.

Then, I looked directly at the three agents and said, "You know the protocol as well as anybody, agents. If someone has an arrest warrant out, they must be brought to the closest CRC facility immediately."

This got the effect I was looking for. All three pulled their NIDs, with one trained on Tavas and two on the other agent.

"Drop your weapon, Shilling," one said. Shilling didn't waste any time putting their gun on the floor. Then, the same agent said, "You too, Captain. We will take you and Shilling to the nearest CRC and clear this up. If it's a misunderstanding, we can be back here in under an hour."

Captain Tavas, now turning quite red with rage, turned back to me and sneered, "I know this was you, and you are going to pay. If you tampered with the warrant system, you will be going away for a long time!"

Then, he glared at the three agents and said to one, "Agent Culig, you stay here and watch Blackwood until we get back. Don't go anywhere near her, no matter what happens." Agent Culig nodded, and the other four members of my interrogation team left.

When they were gone, I turned to Culig. "I think the captain is involved in something nefarious. Don't you think his behavior is strange?"

Culig responded with only, "You're the one whose behavior is strange," and went back to brooding. Okay, I set myself up for that one.

As I waited, I became increasingly anxious, wondering what Libra was going to do about this situation. But I wasn't going to risk asking it out loud just now. Luckily, Libra provided me a quiet update just a couple of minutes later.

"Get ready," was all it said. Lord, it would be nice to have a little more detail on these actions it was undertaking to get me out of here.

Suddenly, my powered manacles opened, and over the PA system, a digital voice exclaimed, "Powered manacle system failure! Please engage the manual system immediately to ensure the prisoner remains restrained!"

Agent Culig, showing obvious panic, started edging toward me and eyeing the large manual engagement lever on the side of the chair. I sat calmly, giving no indication that I would try and escape.

"Blackwood, I am going to reach down beside the chair and pull this lever. If you make any move whatsoever, I will be forced to stun you." I nodded in acceptance.

When Culig got to the side of the chair, he began to squat and glanced briefly downward to locate the lever. That was all the time I needed. Pushing upward with everything I had, I leapt up and landed with my feet on the chair's seat. Then, I quickly pivoted ninety degrees and kneed Culig viciously in the jaw, sending him reeling backward.

Still in a daze, I saw Culig attempting to grab his NID out of its holster, but before he could dislodge the weapon, I was on him with a powerful push kick.

He slammed hard against the wall, and before he could recover, I gripped hard around his throat with one hand while I pulled the NID from its holster. Then I stepped back and trained the gun on his chest.

"Culig, I have no interest in using this, so please come and sit in the chair," I stated, trying to convey the truth in what I was saying.

Culig was nodding, but I saw his eyes start to narrow, and suddenly he was rushing toward me. Not interested in taking any chances, I pulled the trigger at full power and watched Culig flop to the ground, twitching violently. He was out cold almost immediately.

Fuck, this was just what I had wanted to avoid. Tavas was going to have a field day now that I had assaulted a CAD agent.

Knowing I didn't have any time to wallow, I fished through Culig's pockets until I located his shuttle fob. Then I left the interrogation room as fast as I could and sprinted down the hall toward the war room.

"Libra, please tell me the next part of your plan is playing the surveillance footage from outside Johril's apartment," I said, feeling panicked. We didn't have a lot of time before the other agents would be heading back.

"Of course!" said Libra proudly. "The holo is active now and awaiting your presence before commencing!"

I burst into the war room just as the surveillance started to play on a large holo in the middle of the room. The tech services shuttle was at the center of the holo, right outside Johril's apartment. Aeon and the other female EdgeKind were standing by the cab, holding their tool kits. Just then, I barged out of the front door and straight into the shuttle. I pushed past Aeon and down the street, as the two EdgeKind watched on. They shared a quick glance, got into their seats, rose up to about five meters in altitude, and began to fly north.

Over the next several minutes, as I tracked the shuttle, the surveillance footage kept jumping from street cam to street cam, creating a patchwork of different angles and vantages. It was taking way too long, so I told Libra to speed it up to 5x, which I assume was relayed on to Sentinel.

After a few more minutes of this, Aeon and his companion landed in front of a glass building and exited the shuttle, heading toward the front door. I gasped. This was the office of Benevora Biotech.

Just then, Libra stated forcefully, "Freya, Captain Tavas and the other agents have been cleared by CRC and are heading back here now. You need to leave immediately."

Dammit, if I had another hour or so, I could find out where Aeon headed after his visit to Benevora. Since this footage was from more than six months ago, there would be no point going there now, especially without any solid evidence of their involvement in the conspiracy.

While this had all been a shocking revelation and probably useful intel in a conversation with Aeon, I had now lost a very valuable head start on Tavas and Collections, so there was a very real chance I may never end up confronting him.

I left the war room and ran out the front door, using Culig's fob to locate his shuttle. I grinned slightly when I realized it was a high-powered interceptor, much faster than that piece of shit I had boosted prior to my arrest. At least I'd have a chance this time.

As I lifted up to ten meters and started heading east, I saw the analysts approaching the office. I had to haul ass, as there would be an arrest warrant out anytime now.

I stayed at standard altitude and speed while within city limits, not wanting to attract any unwanted attention. I realized I was glancing at my rearview display obsessively, like a meerkat on lookout, but so far, no one was following me.

Once I was outside city limits, I opened up the throttle to three-quarter burn (any faster and I would have had to stop to refuel before getting to The Fringe) and followed the large, slow-moving Oxford River toward the mountains.

It was still night, but a huge glowing moon sat heavy in the sky, illuminating The Bowl in all its splendor. The Bowl was mainly utilized for agricultural purposes, and its unique, stained-glasslike design was striking from this vantage. Each field was a unique, amoebic shape and separated from its neighbors by fifty-meter-wide corridors of mature mixed forest. Multipurpose trails ran down the center of each corridor, and citizens could get lost (in a good way) hiking or biking along the hundreds of kilometers of trails while enjoying the gorgeous scenery along the way.

I passed out of The Bowl and took the eastern passage through the TB10M mountain range, which was a hundred kilometers out from the capital. Next, I would need to cross the curved valley known as TB1020V.

I hadn't spent too much time in TB1020V, having grown up in the next valley out (2030), but it was your typical CiviLibran mix of agriculture, manufacturing, mining, forestry, energy production (which was almost entirely nuclear fusion and solar based), and systematically located towns and cities. However, it wasn't as industrial in appearance as it might sound. CiviLibran design rules required a heavy dose of green architecture and natural landscapes, to ensure its people enjoyed looking out their windows and were motivated to get outdoors and live a healthy lifestyle.

It took me about an hour to get across TB1020V to the next mountain pass, and I still hadn't noticed anyone tailing me. I was actually starting to feel my shoulders relax a bit, thinking that maybe, just maybe, I had gotten enough of a jump to make it to The Fringe before Collections caught up to me. This feeling of ease increased even more as I entered my home valley, with the sun just coming up over the mountains.

I had spent the vast majority of my life in TB2030V prior to joining the DD (besides a few short stints with my mother in Novaluxia) and knew almost every square kilometer of it. Whether it was exploring the abundant wilderness, helping my father at the manufacturing plant, or working odd jobs around the valley, I had loved my time here, and definitely got that feeling of being home as soon as I left the pass. Wanting to see as much of it as I could, I rose up to one hundred meters in altitude so I could take it all in. I realized immediately that it had been a mistake.

Whether or not the four-agent Collections shuttle would have noticed me if I had stayed low, I can't say, but as soon as I hit the higher altitude, I could see them a few kilometers back, pushing hard at full burn. Knowing there was no point in dropping back down now, I also went into full burn, trying to get across the valley as quickly as possible. My shuttle was fast, to be sure, but not as fast as that rocket they were flying. I wasn't going to make it.

I knew I was about twenty kilometers from my father's old plant and the forested area around it, so I made a quick course correction and started heading in that direction.

To Libra, I said, "How long before they are on us? Can we make it to the plant?"

"Yes, but barely," Libra responded. "Do you have a plan?"

"I think so, but it's not a great one."

As I started to approach the plant, I dropped to an altitude just above the forest canopy, maintaining full burn. I was heading for a small clearing, about two kilometers away. Not willing to switch into auto mode, I maintained control while searching the glove box for antenna-removing gear. It was empty.

"Libra, I am going to need your help," I said, praying it would be able to come through on this. "Are you able to keep my location broadcasting from the shuttle after I leave it?" Vehicles, bots, and CiviLibrans all contained location beacons, which broadcast their coordinates at all times. Since a vehicle's broadcasting power was much greater than a human's, whenever someone entered a shuttle, their own broadcast switched over to the vehicle's, to ensure the best possible signal was available while they were inside. I was going to try to use that to my advantage.

Libra paused, then said, "Yes, but only for a short time. When you start to leave the shuttle, I can force a system update for your own location/navigation services, which will put your beacon offline. While this is happening, your position will continue to appear like it is inside the shuttle."

"What do you mean by a short time?" I asked, wanting to have as good an idea as possible about whether this was going to work.

"About two minutes." Not great, but it would have to do.

I came across the tree line to the clearing I was after, put the thrusters hard in reverse, and dropped down just inside the wall of trees. Then I jumped out and started running toward the farm bot plant as fast as I could. It would take me about five minutes to get there.

Behind me, I heard the big Collections shuttle come roaring across the tree line, hovering above my shuttle for a few seconds before coming to a landing a few dozen meters away. My hope was that they would think I was making a stand here, using the NID I had taken from Culig to try to neutralize them before continuing on.

I was about a kilometer from the plant when I heard their shuttle take off. They must have just received my actual location data. I burst out into the facility's yard and made a beeline toward the front entrance as I heard the shuttle approaching behind me. They were just beginning their descent as I ran through the door.

In the lobby, I looked around frantically until luckily making eye contact with Lumi, who was just coming out of her office. Lumi and my father had worked together for years, and I spent a lot of time at her family's home growing up.

"Freya, what are you doing here?" Lumi asked, clearly alarmed by the incoming Collections shuttle and my obvious state of panic.

"Lumi, I need your help!" I hollered, knowing I had very little time. "I am in the middle of some kind of conspiracy and am on my way to confront Aeon Strider. But these Collections assholes have no interest in letting me get there."

At the name Aeon Strider, Lumi's expression darkened. She had been at the plant when the EdgeKind had attacked, leaving my father and several more of her friends dead. "What do you need?"

"In less than a minute, there will be four agents barging through those doors. I need you to stall them while one of the other supervisors disables their shuttle. While that is happening, I will sprint back to my own shuttle and head to The Fringe."

"Sure, we can make that happen for you, sweetie." Lumi grinned. "But promise you will come back for a drink once things cool down. We hardly see you anymore!"

Giving Lumi a quick hug, I whispered, "I promise."

I headed for the side door, and as soon as I heard an agent speaking to Lumi, I took off back toward my shuttle. Even if Lumi and her crew were able to get the job done, I knew Collections would still end up taking one of the supervisor's vehicles; however, I was very confident that I would have no problem outrunning one of those shit cans.

Sure enough, as I rose up to thirty meters and tore across the open space above the plant, I could see a Collections agent yelling at Lumi while another tried to start their shuttle. "Good ol' Lumi," I said, grinning to myself.

Chapter 5

The rest of the trip out to The Fringe was surprisingly uneventful. Of course, I knew the Collections agents were still in pursuit, but even with a stop to refuel and pick up some supplies, they had come nowhere near to catching up with my interceptor.

The further out into the higher-numbered TerraBands I went, the more sparsely populated they became. The landscape flora also became less mature, since those areas had been terra-detailed more recently.

As I approached TB70M mountain range, I began to see the telltale signs of the terra-detailing work that was well underway along The Fringe. Soil-hauling transport bots, like massive bucket-wearing tortoises, plodded slowly toward their destinations, their long journeys from the algae-composting facilities near the coast almost complete.

Traveling on, smaller bots became visible along the foothills of the mountain range, busy performing the detailing work they were known for. The rock grinders were the largest of the group and the first to work an area, flattening out the jagged, uneven surfaces and filling in any crevices as they went. Soil spreaders came next, always within a few dozen meters from a soil transport, adding the organic rich medium crucial for plant growth. Last came the aerial seeders, flying at low altitudes and spreading first grass seed (to inhibit erosion), then larger plant and tree seeds depending on the planned ecosystem.

There weren't many humans out here, with the approved bot-to-human ratio being in the 50-to-1 range, however supervisors were easy to pick out, hovering higher than the bots in their observation shuttles. I'm sure they were wondering what a CAD interceptor was doing out here, seven hundred kilometers from the capital, but I knew that type well, and they preferred to keep to themselves.

Coming out of the mountain pass, the TB7080V valley came into view, and seeing it was like emerging onto a different planet. The land was desolate, covered in jagged gray rock as far as the eye could see. Huge scrapes and gouges were visible all along the valley floor and into the next mountain range, a result of the terraforming work done centuries ago. The ancient machines that had created the recurring mountain/valley ring pattern had been composed of both above- and below-ground earth-moving equipment, unfathomably large in size. The most impressive were the trio of mole-like plows that operated below ground and which created the mountain ranges. The center mole was an earth lifter, and it was enormous. At over eight kilometers wide and a kilometer tall, it was essentially there to push a huge wedge-shaped vertical plow, which lifted the mountains straight out of the ground. To ensure that the millions of tons of lifted rock did not simply collapse back into place once the center mole passed, it was flanked by two four-kilometer-wide crawlers that pushed horizontal plow blades, backfilling the void left by the lifter. All this shifting of earth had quite an effect on the areas just below the foothills, so massive above-ground earth movers remained busy filling voids and cutting the lakes and rivers that dotted the valleys today.

Before leaving the shuttle, I reluctantly plotted a course for the autopilot to follow, along The Fringe's perimeter all the way to the western ocean south of Novaluxia. As much as I wanted to have a vehicle here to return home in when or if I came back, it would essentially act as a homing beacon for Collections to follow, and even though I wouldn't be here when they arrived, it would certainly make the chances of them finding me much higher.

Watching the shuttle fly off, I imagined I was feeling (to a small degree, anyway) like the C6 pioneers when their ship was finally dismantled. There was definitely no going back now, so I better get my shit together and figure this out.

Following my mother's vague instructions, I walked along the foothills north of the pass for about a kilometer, wondering how the hell I was going to figure out where Aeon was. With the way the mountains had been created, the earth beneath was like Swiss cheese, made up of thousands of fissures, caverns, and caves, likely thousands of cubic kilometers in volume. It was an enormous maze you could easily get lost in, wandering around until you died of dehydration.

Seeing this strange landscape reminded me of the day I was gifted that bottomless well of favors, a.k.a. the day I saved Trace's life. It didn't happen in this exact spot, of course; it was probably a few hundred kilometers south of here if I had to guess, but it could have been the same place, based on its very similar appearance.

We were following a lead we had received concerning the possible location of an EdgeKind tunnel entrance, thought to be near the base of the range. While traversing the typical jagged rocks in the area, Trace had slipped and fallen some ten meters down into a narrow gorge. The sound of him hitting the bottom made me sick to my stomach.

"Trace!" I'd yelled down into the gorge. He was motionless.

I quickly took my pack off, only to have my heart sink when I realized Trace had the rope.

With no time to spare, I pressed my hands and feet against both sides of the gorge like a snow angel and slid down way too fast. Even though I had gloves, my hands were torn up by the time I hit bottom.

I rushed over to Trace's lifeless body and started to panic when I saw that one of his femurs was sticking out through the skin. He was bleeding pretty heavily, but it didn't appear he'd pierced the carotid artery. Thank God.

I quickly prepared a crude tourniquet, but just as I was finishing tying it, I heard a shuffling sound behind me. Jumping up, I pulled my NID and turned quickly, training the weapon in that direction.

There stood two EdgeKind, brandishing stun pikes.

"Easy," I said softly. "No need for violence. My friend here is hurt badly, and I need to get him to a surgeon." They glanced down at Trace before returning their intense gazes to me.

"Why are you here?" one asked.

"I just told you."

"No, I mean why are you both here?"

"Look, that doesn't matter now. I have no interest in following you. I'm leaving here with my friend, and I promise you we'll never return."

"I don't believe you."

I paused, then tossed my NID out in front of them.

"His too."

When they'd picked up both of our NIDs, the tension finally eased a bit. After I'd tied Trace onto my back, they even showed me an easier way to get out of the gorge.

"I want you to promise you'll never return, and to remember that we let you go, the next time you're on a mission," was the last thing they'd said, as I was climbing up onto the surface. I'd nodded in agreement.

Of course, as soon as I'd gotten Trace back to base, I'd gathered a small force and returned, only to find the cave they'd been standing in had been blasted shut.

I'd convinced myself that my lack of honor was okay. After all, they hadn't believed me anyway, and also, they were just EdgeKind. Still, I'd never been able to truly get over it.

And now here I was, planning to enter their home uninvited, a CiviLibran they despised more than possibly any other.

I was the one they referred to as Dreadmother.

After another kilometer of carefully navigating the rocks and gazing down into the abyss, trying to decide which one led to Aeon, I heard a noise far behind me and turned, tensing. There appeared to be a shuttle coming out of the pass, moving very quickly.

I ducked behind an outcropping of rock, and squinting hard, realized what it was: the damn Collections shuttle.

"Jesus, those guys are like flies to shit," I mumbled, realizing immediately that my role in this particular metaphor was less than flattering. "Or should I say, bees to honey."

I had expected them to be too impatient to wait and fix their shuttle, but apparently, I had been wrong. Strategically, they had definitely made the right choice. With their vehicle being over twice as fast as the commuter version, they had easily made up any lost time caused by waiting for the repair.

They slowed from their blistering pace once in line with the foothills, increased their altitude, and turned south, following the shuttle's path I had sent that way. I breathed a sigh of relief, watching them fade into the distance. But then, a couple of kilometers into their journey south, they did a 180 and started coming back in my direction. *Dammit.*

My location beacon accuracy would be pretty shoddy this far out, but with enough time, the agents would definitely pin me down, especially if they lucked out and passed by close enough on this run north. I needed to get underground right now.

Peering down a nearby gorge, I could see that about a hundred meters away, it transitioned into more of a small cave that led into the mountain. I dropped down about three meters, and moving quickly, headed toward the hole. As I ran, I tried my comm to check in with Libra one last time, but there was no connection. "See you on the other side, my favorite sociopath," I said aloud, sighing.

As I reached the hole, I realized how small it was—definitely too small for me to crawl through with my backpack on. So, I took off the pack and pushed it in, then wriggled through in a prone position. Luckily, the hole opened up a bit on the other side, and after grabbing my bag, I was able to pick up the pace just as I heard the shuttle go past overhead.

I paused, listening hard, and again my heart sank. The shuttle had come to a hovering position right above me and sounded like it was decreasing its altitude. Knowing I needed to create as much distance as possible before the agents were in the mountain with me, I flicked on my headlamp and started moving quickly—as quickly as is possible in a narrow, unknown cave system—while heading deeper into the mountain.

I had been traveling for at least thirty minutes and making good time. The cave was actually becoming a bit wider and far taller. In fact, it had to be a good forty meters to the peak at this point, more of a cavern really. Eventually, I came to a spot where the cave split in two, however, the secondary route was much smaller and appeared to get tighter as it went, at least as far as I could make out through the gloom. So, I made the decision to stay on the main artery I was currently traveling.

After another fifteen minutes or so, I started to worry I had made the wrong decision. The cave was beginning to pinch in dramatically, and I had to turn sideways to get through.

Then abruptly, it ended. *Fuck!*

"Stars may be hidden, but they always shine," I mumbled to myself. It was a saying my father used during challenging times. Strangely, speaking it always provided a small measure of relief when I needed it most.

I figured I still had time to make it back to the split, so I turned around and moved as fast as I could back the way I had come. I was feeling pretty nimble now that I had my cave legs (is that a thing?) and entered the wide cavern section just before the fork in a hair under ten minutes.

Then I saw them.

There were two Collections agents about fifty meters ahead of me, coming in my direction. The other two must have split off. I ducked quickly behind a narrow outcropping of rock, waiting anxiously to see if they'd noticed me. When they started talking, it became clear they definitely had.

"Freya Blackwood," one called out. "We are here to collect you and return you to MaxSec2, as you have not yet completed your sentence."

I stayed quiet, so the agent continued. "Now, I know you have made visual contact with two of us, but I can assure you there are two more on their way here now. You have no chance against four experienced Collections agents. Please come out, and we won't hurt you. Our job is to return you safely to the CRC facility."

It took me a second to realize why this Collections agent, member of a group infamous for their unnerving silence during arrests, was being so chatty. It was a distraction. While they were blathering away, I was sure the second was creeping ever closer to my position and would pop out at any second and stun me at full power. I did some quick math and determined I had about thirty seconds until the agent made their move.

While I counted down, I readied my own weapon and got into a squat position. Ten seconds now.

Once I got to zero, I popped up as explosively as I could, and even though I was expecting the agent to be close, I was shocked to find them mere centimeters from my face—and by the way the agent froze, I was guessing they were as surprised as me. Luckily, I was the first to recover.

Using my handheld NID, I backhanded the agent hard in the face, then shoved them backward with all my strength. The agent stumbled a few feet, and before they could recover, I fired my weapon at full power directly into their chest. The agent went down hard, and I ducked back down behind the rock.

"That was not very smart, Ms. Blackwood," said the chatty agent, starting to sound irritated. "Assaulting a Collections agent will result in at least another five hundred rehab simulations added to your sentence."

I heard footsteps, then voices speaking quietly. The agent continued, "My colleagues have arrived now, and we are going to begin circling you. I know you reached a dead end further down the cave, otherwise you would not have returned. You have no way to escape."

The cave became eerily silent, and I knew Collections were beginning to make their move. I took a deep breath, preparing for the ensuing battle. I had decided some time ago that I wasn't going to go back without a fight, and there was no way I was adjusting that strategy now. I started to count backward from ten.

... five, four, three, two, one.

Just as I was about to jump up, I heard yelling and the distinct sound of arcing electricity. There was a fight going on in the cave.

Peeking out from behind the rock, I was surprised to see at least a dozen new faces in the gloom. Some were carrying NID's, while others brandished long stun pikes, electricity sparking angrily at their tips. The NID carriers were standing back, weapons trained on the Collections agents, while those holding pikes were in tight, stabbing and swinging furiously.

The agents fought heroically, disarming and stunning several of the cave people, but they were badly outnumbered. In the end, all four (counting my important contribution) lay unconscious on the floor, while their attackers stood panting around them.

I thought to myself, *maybe they don't know I am here*, just seconds before a gravelly voice called out, "Toss your weapon, and come out from behind the rock, or we will put you down like these ones." Sighing, I threw my NID out onto the cave floor and stood, taking in the scene.

I recognized the speaker immediately. It was the woman who had been with Aeon outside Johril's apartment.

No doubt noticing my surprised expression, the woman said, "Freya Blackwood, you made a mistake coming here."

"You know my name, now give me yours," I demanded in turn, trying to sound less afraid than I was feeling.

"My name is Corinna Vos, and I am charged with keeping your kind from entering this place."

I started walking out toward Corinna, before stating, "I am here to speak with Aeon Strider. Please take me to him."

Corinna and the others began laughing, but it was not friendly. She said, "You do not make demands here, Dreadmother."

Before I could respond, Vos nodded to five pike carriers near me, who immediately started closing in, weapons raised and crackling. The first to arrive stabbed at my chest, but I moved laterally just in time, grabbing the staff as it went past. I quickly disarmed my attacker, turned the weapon around, and jammed it into his neck, causing him to scream and fall to the ground.

Another was on me already. I parried her attack and was beginning my own thrust when I felt a searing pain in my back, then another in my side. I turned to see two pikes held hard against me and knew what would come next. My leg muscles went first, and I crumbled to the ground, spasming violently. The last thing I remembered as my vision started to darken was Corinna standing above me, giving the command to tie me up and throw me in the mine cart with the others.

...

I awoke in a cell.

Well, it was more of a cage, if I am being honest. Looking around, I could see there were dozens more like the one I was in, four of which held the Collections agents. All were awake and glaring at me with contempt.

The cages were situated in a large rock chamber, probably twenty meters wide by fifty meters tall. It was surprisingly well lit, by way of dozens of industrial-type lights fastened to the rock ceiling. A few guards milled about.

To the Collections agents I said, "Looks like we are all criminals now. I guess that means we're on the same team?" They all just scowled at me. Even the chatty one was brooding in silence.

While waiting for whatever was coming next, I tried to take stock of my situation. This was certainly not how I expected the operation to play out, but considering the Collections agents were no longer a threat, and I had located someone I knew was close with Aeon, things could really have been a lot worse. To be honest, when I had entered the cave, I had given myself an eighty percent chance of either being collected or becoming lost and dying of starvation somewhere under the mountain. This was a decent start really.

Probably noticing me grinning to myself, one of the agents asked, "What are you so happy about, Blackwood? Do you really expect that we are getting out of here alive? The EdgeKind only survive by staying to the shadows, hidden from CiviLibrans. There is no way they will risk letting us go."

My short-lived grin faded. This was definitely an accurate projection of our future. "Buzzkill," I mumbled, now frowning.

It was several hours before I saw Corinna come into the chamber, flanked by a few guards. She approached my cage. "Blackwood, you are coming with us."

After my hands were bound, I was forced along roughly into another, smaller chamber, where a tall man stood behind an unpainted metal table. It was Aeon Strider.

"Appreciate you complying with my demand, Vos," I said, staring at my captor. She just gave me a look like she wanted to beat me down right then and there.

Having only gotten a quick look at Aeon during my escape, I had not realized how dramatic the man was in appearance. He was over two meters tall, and while he wasn't heavily muscled like I was, his lean, wiry frame was clearly strong. He had dark walnut skin, a black beard, and eyes that were a striking green-gold color. His gaze was intelligent, discerning.

After I was pushed into a simple chair across from Strider, he sat down, while Corinna took a standing position beside him, staring hard at me. She couldn't have been more physically different from Aeon. Short and powerful in build, she was plain in appearance and probably fifteen years older than he was. However, like Aeon, she'd clearly lived a hard life.

Aeon was the first to speak. "As I'm sure you are aware, you have quite the infamous reputation in these parts, Dreadmother. That, and the trouble you and your agents caused out in the caves, are difficult things to ignore. Now, I must decide how to punish you."

"Aeon, you sit here acting haughtily toward me when we both know you have been sneaking around Novaluxia, taking a central role in the murder of innocent people. Fuck you and your judgment."

Strider, knowing he had the upper hand, decided wisely not to take the bait, and instead asked, "Are you familiar with a large DD operation that took place about twenty-five years ago in the TB6070V valley?"

"Of course, we learned about it during training," I responded. "DD scouts located an EdgeKind war camp in the valley and neutralized it before your forces could begin their assault."

Strider and Vos both scowled at my rendition of the event. "You were lied to, Blackwood. It wasn't a war camp; it was a settlement."

"Bullshit."

"I was there," continued Aeon. "We both were." At that, he nodded toward Corinna.

Aeon began to tell the story of SunHold, a small above-ground settlement built in defiance of CiviLibra's Defense Division, where some three hundred EdgeKind, tired of living like moles under the ground, had decided to build their new home.

"I was around five years old when they came," began Aeon. "I and some other youths, while under the watchful eye of Corinna here, were out foraging in the woods. Suddenly, we heard the telltale roar of large DD shuttles approaching SunHold and began to make our way back, as quickly as we could.

"When we reached the clearing, we were horrified by what they saw. The DD, which was already gone, had dropped dozens of canisters of Somniacide gas, and the whole settlement was already suffering the effects of the drug.

"Somniacide, by its nature, makes you terrified that everything is trying to kill you, and so if anything comes close, you lash out in defense. Now, imagine a whole town suffering the same effects, all in tight proximity, and thinking the others are all demons and beasts out for blood. It was carnage."

He paused, and the expressions of pain on both his and Corinna's faces revealed the profound trauma of the event.

"Corinna took us children away as quickly as possible, back to our old underground colony, while we all cried and begged for our parents. As it turned out, mine, like so many others, were already dead."

The image was painful to imagine, and with the way Aeon was describing it, I could not bring myself to believe he was lying.

"I'm sorry," was all I could mutter.

"While I do appreciate you saying that, Freya," replied Aeon, "your words have no power to bring back my parents."

"What do you want from me?" I asked, uncomfortable with this current theme and wanting to get to the point.

"You might be surprised to learn that I am actually interested in negotiating with you," Aeon replied. This was encouraging.

He continued, "However, there would be mutiny if I were to do so without punishing you in some way first, considering the pain you and your people have caused my own."

Oh shit, never mind. I knew what was coming before even seeing the needle.

"Assuming you don't devolve into one of the DreamWrought, in a few days, I'll meet you back here, so we can continue our discussion," said

Aeon, standing. I saw Corinna lifting a needle from a small case on the table and admiring it, clearly for effect.

"There has to be another way, Aeon," I said softly, mouth dry.

Aeon just held up his hand. "I think this will help to ensure our negotiations are productive actually, what with you having firsthand knowledge of what it feels like to suffer as we all have. It's good to come at these things with a similar mindset."

I was sweating now, severely dreading what was coming.

I saw someone moving toward me from the side, but before I could duck, they were holding my head in place. Another came forward with a small device and held it against my neural implant antenna. I heard a high-pitched whine, and then my HUD flickered out. *Not again.*

"Just in case you harbor any hopes of letting Libra know where you are," said Corinna. "Not that you'll have any connection down here."

"Down here?" I asked. "Aren't you going to leave me out in The Waste?"

Corinna smiled darkly. "No, Dreadmother, our version of the treatment comes with a bit of a regional twist."

Chapter 6

Corinna's guards dragged me kicking and screaming to an autonomous mine cart, where they blindfolded me, threw me in the back, and tied me to the guardrail for good measure.

Our journey was long, slow, and brutally rough, but I did my best to remember every turn we made, thinking I might possibly have time to work my way back before the worst of the Somniacide kicked in.

Eventually we stopped, and I was thrown to the ground unceremoniously. Corinna herself removed my blindfold.

"Well, here we are," she said sweetly, pulling the needle out of its carrying case for the second time today.

While she prepared the injection, she reminisced. "You know, I still remember my first Somniacide injection. I was probably around fourteen and was out with a small crew, stealing vegetables from one of your fields."

I really didn't care to hear this story at the moment and told Corinna as much. She ignored me.

"I remember the DD shuttles appearing as if out of nowhere; it happened so fast," she continued. "Even though we were all just scared teenagers, they treated us brutally, setting their NIDs to low power, to ensure we wouldn't pass out as they stunned us over and over."

That was pretty typical behavior by the DD, to be honest, unnecessary as it was.

"Once we were out in The Waste and injected, all hell broke loose. The visions began almost immediately, and I remember my friends turning into monsters before my eyes, all seemingly intent on tearing me to pieces.

"A few, like me, scattered and ran off into the abyss, but looking back, I could see several of the monsters beating mercilessly on each other, trying to eradicate the perceived threats all around them.

"I was found two days later by some adults from the colony, half dead from dehydration and still suffering from flash hallucinations every few minutes. It took me weeks before I was back to normal—if you're ever truly back to normal once you've been given Somniacide."

Corinna was quiet for a time, then turned and said, "At least be happy that you'll be alone for this, with no chance of killing or being killed by your friends."

It all happened very quickly. In unison, a guard swooped in and stunned me with an NID, leaving me temporarily disoriented and paralyzed, while Corinna injected me in the neck with the Somniacide needle. Then, they untied me, jumped in the cart, and started driving back the way we had come.

I used all my strength to push myself up onto my hands and knees and began crawling slowly toward the cart, now long gone around a bend. I had made it no more than a few meters when an overwhelming sense of existential dread washed over me, leaving me breathless with anticipation of what was coming. There seemed to be a low, ominous hum emanating from all directions.

Just then, I felt a presence enter the cave. It was malevolent, yet invisible, and seemed to be watching me from high above with all the hatred it could gather.

"Come on, you bastards!" I screamed into the air. And they did.

Like huge smoky serpents with mouths full of long teeth, the wraiths came down at me, crashing hard into my body and pushing with a force that drove me to my stomach. I couldn't breathe, and the pressure caused me to start vomiting uncontrollably. The pain from their assault was searing, like being stung by a thousand jellyfish, relentless in its fury.

During my training on the effects of Somniacide, I'd heard that the hallucinations came in waves, providing the victim with momentary periods of relief. There was none for me.

The wraiths, now biting against my skin with their transparent, knifelike teeth, suddenly broke through and were inside me, searching for my soul. The pain was unlike anything I'd ever experienced, an overwhelming burning sensation similar to what my father probably felt as he was dying.

I was howling, immobile on my stomach, vomit all over my cheeks and mouth. Then, as I watched in horror, the wraiths ripped the soul from my body and began devouring it beside me while my energy faded. I was dying.

I sank into an abyss of nothingness, not caring about anything anymore, just happy that the suffering was over.

Then I was back.

The wraiths were gone, as was the pain. I was reborn. *Oh fuck, death was what came at the end of the wave*, I realized. That was my reprieve. My body shook as I sobbed, knowing that I was about to be hit by the next wave.

Suddenly, everything became eerily quiet, like the cave had become a vacuum. The silence was so absolute that all I could hear was an intense, maddening ringing in my ears. I got onto my haunches and hugged my knees tightly, shaking violently. Then I heard it.

It started as a distant vibration every few seconds, shaking the ground beneath me ever so slightly. As it came closer, the vibrations became more of a rumbling sound, and I knew it was coming from further down the cave. I watched in pure horror as a dim red light, full of malice, began illuminating the walls about a hundred meters down the cave.

Then it made its entrance.

It was like a huge hairy crocodile, fur matted and unkempt. Its face was that of a malicious cat, with a tooth-filled mouth spread in a wide, unnerving grin. Its eyes were huge and red, the cause of the glow I had seen. I began to shuffle backward on all fours, trying to get away from this nightmare. But as soon as it locked eyes on me, it started moving forward with unnatural speed, its strange, undulating gait propelling it directly toward me. I tried to stand, but I was still without much strength and stumbled back to the ground. Crawling away, I looked back in horror to see its huge face getting closer and closer at an unbelievable rate.

Then it was on me.

It bit hard onto one of my legs, shaking its head from side to side until it tore free. I roared in pain as it tossed my limb and came back for the next. Working away happily, it ripped both my legs and arms off my bleeding body, then cocked its head as it stared me in the eye.

"My, but you have been naughty, Dreadmother," it seethed, just before it tore off my head.

Wave upon wave of nightmares and deaths followed, until I lost track of all time. From worms devouring my body to schools of vampire bats with the faces of my friends, it was an endless barrage that left me weak and wishing for a real death.

Waking from one particularly awful wave, not twenty meters away, I spotted one of the DreamWrought limping in my direction. It had the face of my father.

Pushing myself onto my feet and steadying myself against a wall, I yelled, "Please, Father, I don't want to hurt you! Leave me in peace!"

But it replied only, "I am not your father, only one who wishes to feast on your body!" With that, it started sprinting toward me.

It barreled straight into me, biting hard into my neck as I bellowed.

"Father, please, do not torment me here!" I begged, pushing the nightmare to the ground.

It gathered itself for another attack.

Though I was dangerously weak, the partial paralysis I had received from being stunned was mostly worn off, so I shuffled as quickly as I could away from this demon version of my father. But it was much faster than I.

It leapt onto my back, and we went crashing to the ground, my head hitting hard against a rock. My vision was spinning.

I rolled away and gathered myself, then kicked the thing hard in the chest. It screamed.

Running again, I heard it get to its feet and tear after me, full of rage and hunger. Suddenly I stopped. There was a cliff directly in front of me.

Turning, I stretched out my arms in a pleading motion, but my father was not slowing. At the last second, I sidestepped, but as it flew past me, it grabbed my arm hard, and we both went flying out into the abyss. Just before I hit the rocks below, I felt relief, knowing that at least another wave was coming to an end.

...

I awoke back in my cage. I was lying on a crude cot, and my head was bandaged. I tried to lift my head up, but the pain was excruciating. I heard a guard say, "Easy there, you are in pretty rough shape," before lying back down.

I looked out at the guard and saw his face shift from humanlike to something satanic, then back again. My body was still trying to rid itself of Somniacide, apparently.

"What the fuck happened?" I asked, grimacing.

"You went over a cliff, that's what happened. Lucky you landed on a ledge halfway down, cause you definitely wouldn't have survived a fall to the bottom. We didn't think you'd move about so much, you see, but you ended up in a pretty dangerous part of the cave. Figured you'd be immobile, what with the stunning you received. Determined big oaf you are."

Jesus, so that last part had been real. It had been impossible to tell the difference between hallucination and reality at that point.

The guard continued, "You're lucky in a way, because you only had to go through about twenty-four hours of the nightmares. You've been unconscious for two days or so." He nodded to some tubes sticking out of my arm. "Had to hook you up to fluids cause you were dry as an old piece of leather when we brought you back. Then you started screaming about your father and thrashing, so we had to give you some anesthesia to keep you under. Wild ride you've had."

"How would you react if a DreamWrought with your father's face tried to kill you?" I snarled in response.

"DreamWrought would never attack like that," he said and went back to his guard duty.

While I was lying there, I glanced around at the other cages. The Collections agents were no longer there.

"What happened to those ones?" I asked, pointing toward where they had once been.

"None of your concern," was all he offered, but I noticed his expression go grim.

I spent the next day or so dealing with flash hallucinations and fretting about what was next for me. I was pretty sure the Collections agents were dead, but why would they have introduced me to Aeon, given me Somniacide in a "safe" part of the cave, and treated my wounds, only to kill me off now? It didn't add up.

After another day in the cage, I was able to stand up, and my IV was now out. To be honest, I was getting pretty bored, and wanted to get on with whatever was next. I also wanted a distraction, so I wouldn't keep reliving the Somniacide deaths over and over in my mind.

Then finally, Aeon came into the cavern and approached my cage.

"Freya, I see you are starting to bounce back," he said. "Tell me, what was your Somniacide experience like? Do you still believe that giving it to my people when they are caught misbehaving is the right course of action?"

This was a topic that I had been struggling with the last few days, and I was a bit annoyed he decided to just jump right into it.

"You know CiviLibra was founded on the belief that physical violence should be limited as much as possible," I answered. "That is why projectile weapons are illegal. How would you dole out punishment if you were in our position?"

"I'm sure there are lots of defense options outside of engaging in psychological warfare with an enemy that is a fraction of your own strength," he countered. "And is giving Somniacide any less violent than beating someone? Would beating someone turn them into a DreamWrought?"

I knew this was not an argument I was going to win, nor did I really want to. While I, along with everyone else in CiviLibra, had been indoctrinated to feel no more empathy for the EdgeKind than one would an ant, the events of the last few months had left me with a lot of doubts. To make matters worse, I was also tormented by my own oversized role in their suffering. So instead, I tried to shift the discussion.

"If you don't want to be treated like an enemy, then why don't you stop acting like one?" I asked, hoping to put Aeon on the back foot for once. "If you ceased your attacks on CiviLibran infrastructure and kept to yourselves, I'm sure the Somniacide attacks would end."

Aeon looked thoughtful, leading me to believe I had gained the upper hand, then said, "And do you think this is really a way for people to live, hiding underground like moles?" At this he gestured to the cavern behind him.

"Anyway," I said, trying yet another new angle, "you keep coming at me and heaping on the guilt when we both know you have blood on your hands. My father died during one of your raids, and I know without a doubt you are heavily involved in the Killwave murders."

At the mention of my father, Aeon's face became sad. "Freya, I am truly sorry about your father," he began. "When I organized that raid, I was very new to all this and had believed that setting a small fire during raids would serve to distract the supervisors from trying to stop us. It worked for a time, but after the fire at your father's plant went out of control and people died, I ordered an end to that strategy."

"But there have been fires since then, and more death," I said, the anger I still had buried deep starting to boil up.

"I know, and that is something that makes me regret the strategy even more. Despite what many CiviLibrans think, I am not some cave king, ruling all Eridanians. In fact, our group only comprises about a third of the entire population. When the other groups saw what success we were having starting fires during raids, it became a popular strategy, one that unfortunately continues to this day."

I was skeptical about whether Aeon was telling the truth or not and wanted to keep digging, but something else had caught my attention. "Why did you refer to your people as Eridanians?" I asked.

"EdgeKind is the name Civilbrans gave us. But we are the original peoples here on Epsilon Eridani b, hence Eridanians."

Original peoples? Was Aeon suggesting they were natives here? Was he insane?

Aeon smiled when he noticed my concerned expression. "Eridanians originate from the terraforming teams. When the work was done, some of the nonaugmented workers hid in the caves until the ships had left, not trusting their leadership enough to see what might be in store for them."

"Are there other remnants of terraforming culture that persist?" I asked, curious.

"A few, yes," Aeon responded. "Names, mainly. Valterra, my

official title as clan leader, was originally given to the overseer of each terraforming crew. Nexterra, which is Corrina's title, was given to the right hand."

This was all interesting, and answered some questions I had long had, but I needed to get back to my main purpose for being here. "Several times now, you've evaded my questions about your involvement with the Killwave murders. I need to understand what is going on and why you're in the middle of it."

Aeon nodded his head a few times, then asked, "If I let you out of this cell, unbound, will you attempt to beat me to death the first chance you get?"

"No. But why let me out?" I was growing tense.

"I promise it will help you understand my involvement in the murders."

I nodded.

Aeon had one of the guards open my cage door and motioned for me to follow him. By leading, he was intending to show me that he trusted me not to jump him, but there were two guards behind me with stun pikes, so I knew his trust only went so far.

We followed what looked to be a drilled tunnel before arriving in another large, natural cavern. It appeared to be a hospital. Actually, it was a psychiatric ward.

Dozens of patients lay on cots, all with their arms and legs strapped down. Some screamed, others cried, and the only quiet ones appeared to be heavily sedated.

Aeon let the scene sink in before saying, "This is our Somniacide treatment center. For patients who have not been able to bounce back as you have."

I turned to look at him, anxiety likely written all over my face. "Are they in the early stages of transitioning into the DreamWrought?"

"Some likely are," said Aeon. "However, we are planning to treat them all before that happens."

Before I could ask any more questions, Aeon again beckoned me to follow him. Passing the rows of cots, we reached the end of the large cavern and ducked into a small cutout room to the side.

The scene brought a smile to Aeon's face, but only confusion to mine. A woman lay on an operating table, clearly sedated, while an operating bot hovered above her, waiting for its next task. The woman's skull was open, and her brain was exposed. A doctor was hunched over, installing tiny fibrous wires, which were connected via a harness to some kind of electronic device. A display was showing a row of amoebic blobs, varying in size, length, and color.

"This woman has been suffering from terrifying hallucinations for weeks," Aeon said, not breaking his gaze from the scene. "Without this procedure, she would soon break, never again finding her way home to this reality we all share."

"What is being done to save her?" I asked, nodding to the procedure taking place.

"The technology I was given for my role in the Killwave murders allows for selective removal of memories, in this case, the traumatizing events that occurred from exposure to Somniacide," Aeon explained. "Simply put, those colorful shapes on the screen indicate the intensity and types of emotions experienced during her memories, and the timescale along the bottom gives us the ability to narrow down on those we are sure are the culprits. The colors correspond to the more intense emotions, such as fear, anger, happiness, stress, and love. In this case, we are only interested in fear, anger, and stress, of course."

This sounded eerily similar to the work that Dr. Ellis was working on. "I'm surprised you just admitted to being involved in the murders."

Aeon shrugged. "Like I said, I want to negotiate with you, and to do so, we need to trust each other. Plus, once you leave here, I can guarantee you'll never find me again. Unless I want you to, that is." At this, he gave me a sly grin.

Just then, I heard the doctor say to her patient, "Can you tell me about your favorite childhood memory?"

"Why did she ask that?" I whispered to Aeon.

"It's very important not to be thinking about the memories that are being removed during the process, because doing so can be very stressful for the patient. It's almost like pieces of yourself are being removed while you watch. Furthermore, once the memory is gone, you are instead left with this unsettling feeling of loss, like being incomplete, and it can stick with you indefinitely."

That sounded terrifying. "Who developed this technology?" I asked.

Aeon frowned before responding, "Benevora, I assume, but I am not totally sure."

I sighed before continuing. "Aeon, if we are going to trust each other, I need to know everything about the Killwave murders."

"I understand," he began. "From the beginning?"

"Yes, everything."

Aeon began telling me about how he was approached by two agents, who offered him the memory-removal technology in exchange for taking on key field responsibilities concerning Killwave and supporting Benevora through Oriel Rahm.

"So, what, you were given some names and then went to their apartments and injected them with the virus?" I asked.

"Yes, but it's much more complicated than that," responded Aeon, probably realizing I knew much less than he had assumed. "Freya, the virus is benign. Its role is only to make the public believe it creates murderers so that Benevora can sell vaccines."

My mind was spinning, and with the trace amounts of Somniacide still floating around in my body, I was having a really hard time wrapping my head around all this.

"So then, what caused me to murder Johril?" I asked.

Aeon stared hard at me before responding. "You didn't kill Johril, Freya. It was Corinna."

I felt anger boiling up within me, and my hands clenched into fists. I was going to kill that bitch, and not quickly.

"Freya, don't do anything stupid," Aeon was saying, as his guards began to raise their stun pikes. "Let me finish."

I unclenched my fists, still thinking of the different ways I would make Corinna suffer when I saw her again.

Aeon continued. "The same technology I just showed you is what allowed the Killwave plan to work, with one key addition. While this version allows only for the removal of specific memories, the one we used during the Killwave operations allowed for the addition of new memories to the patient's brain."

I stayed quiet, so Aeon continued. "Essentially, each operation went like this: Corinna and I would sneak into the apartment, office, etc. We'd then threaten the future murder victim to keep quiet while we waited for the fall guy, telling them we wouldn't hurt them if they did what we asked. After the fall guy arrived and settled in, we'd stun them at full power to render them unconscious, then inject them with the Killwave virus. Once the fall guy was out, either Corinna or I would commit the murder by strangling the victim, and then download the firsthand memory of the event onto the device. We would then upload that memory into the fall guy's brain via their neural implant port, and finally stage the fall guy on top of the victim and get out of there before the they woke up and realized what they had done."

The systematic way Aeon was explaining the operation's details was making me nauseous. I had not suspected any of the things he was telling me right now, and it was overwhelming.

"This explains why the timestamps don't align," I mumbled, thinking of what Libra had told me. God I'd love to be able to talk to that arrogant AI about this right now.

Aeon raised his eyebrows. "How do you know about that?" he asked. "Libra told me."

"Interesting. Oriel was concerned about the misalignment between the time of murder and the fall guy's artificial memory of the event. However, she assumed that since the cases would be so open and shut, no deeper analysis would be performed."

I just shrugged, then asked, "Is the operation complete now?"

"Yes," answered Aeon, sounding relieved. "Our agreement ended when vaccination rates reached ninety-eight percent, which as you know, corresponded with Oriel and the rest of the leadership team at Benevora receiving the second part of their CiVal bonus."

Those greedy, corrupt pieces of shit.

I was considering digging into why Aeon seemed so cold about the murders he'd committed, but I knew it would just come across as hypocritical. I didn't imagine he probably felt any more empathy toward CiviLibrans than we did toward his people.

"So, what exactly is it you want from me?" I asked instead.

Aeon nodded. "I need something from you in exchange for the proof you are looking for." With that, he held up the small holoprojector he had been carrying in his pocket. "But I have other matters I need to attend to now, so we will have to reconvene in the morning. You are free to move about in the public spaces and grab a cot in one of the free rooms. I'd recommend keeping your guard up, though, as not everyone is as forgiving of your violent past as I. While I've warned the colony that any aggression toward you will be punished, some might believe that is an acceptable price to pay." With that, he turned and walked off with one of the guards.

The second guard looked at me and said, "Follow me, I will show you to your room."

"What's your name?" I asked, genuinely curious.

"Erasmus Cain."

I followed Erasmus through a series of caves and tunnels, receiving quite a few unkind looks from passers-by. Aeon was right; I was not welcome here.

Entering a tall, narrow cavern, I looked around in awe at the dozens of rows of doors along both of its sides, going up at least fifty meters. Ladders and scaffolding allowed for access to each one.

Erasmus took me up to the fifth level, opened a door with the key he was holding, and handed it to me.

"I'd recommend keeping this locked when you are inside," he said. "Like Valterra Strider told you, there are many that harbor ill will toward you. I'll be back in a couple hours to show you to the mess hall." At that, he turned and climbed down the scaffolding and left the cavern.

I went inside my room and locked the door behind me. It was small, and by the appearance of the rock, seemed like it had been built using a combination of boring and chiseling to create its surfaces.

It was actually quite cozy (or maybe I just felt protected), and I especially appreciated its closed walls after being locked in a cage for several days. Still, it didn't take long to start feeling lonely, surrounded by people who despised me, hundreds of meters under a mountain. I missed Trace most of all.

I worried about how he thought of me now, after my latest series of indiscretions. While he had stuck with me after the Johril murder, since then I had assaulted a CAD agent, become a fugitive, and I'm sure the division was becoming increasingly concerned that I had killed the Collections team they had sent after me.

If only I could see him, I'd be able to explain everything. The problem was, he'd be under watch, and if I tried to meet with him, I was sure it wouldn't be long before a new Collections team would come bursting out of the woodwork and arrest me. Problem for another day, I suppose.

Lying on my cot, I dozed off and dreamed fitfully, probably due to the combination of Somniacide exposure and the mountains of baggage I was carrying around.

In the morning, Erasmus came and took me to the mess hall for breakfast.

"Grab some grub and pick a seat," said Erasmus. "I'll stick with you here to deter anyone from trying anything." With that, he puffed up his chest, causing me to smirk slightly. I'm sure he looked like a child beside me.

I was pleasantly surprised to find mushrooms on the menu, plus fresh fish and sauerkraut. Erasmus was telling me that everything was grown or raised in the cave system.

"Do you have much electrical power?" I asked.

"Yes," was all he offered. I decided not to push for more details.

Breakfast involved looking around at the hundreds of faces in the room and trying to count how many wanted to kill me. It was about ninety percent, no surprise there. What did surprise me was that a small percentage actually seemed curious by my presence, almost in awe. I wondered if the stories of my Somniacide experience had softened their opinion of me somewhat.

After I'd finished, we sat for a few minutes, until I saw Erasmus look up toward one of the entrances. I turned around to see Aeon and Corinna coming toward us. Everyone else in the room seemed to be watching them as well.

"I trust you ate well and slept like shit?" Aeon asked, grinning.

"That's a very accurate assessment of my experience, yes," I responded.

Aeon beckoned me to follow, and we headed back to the cavern where I had first met him. Corinna and I shared an unfriendly glance.

Once we were seated, Aeon began speaking. "With this holoprojector, I believe you have what you need to move to the next phase of your investigation. While I strongly believe there are more layers to this conspiracy than what I am aware of, this footage of a discussion I had with Oriel Rahm will allow you to start to peel the next layer, which starts with questioning her."

"Thank you, Aeon. I appreciate your help in this," I said. "Now, what will this be costing me?"

Aeon looked at Corinna before responding. "Yes, as you have surmised, there is a cost to all this, and that cost is a heavy one. I need you to get the use of Somniacide banned."

My mouth dropped open, shocked at how enormous a request this actually was. "That's not possible," was all I said.

"We believe it is possible," countered Corinna. "With what you know and what you've seen, we think the public outrage that would come from learning about your experiences would force the upper divisions to cease using that poison during DD operations."

I just shook my head, still shocked by what they were asking of me.

"Look," said Aeon, seeing the doubt on my face, "if you are not up to it, fine. We'll just remove your memories of this place and drop you off near Novaluxia. It's your choice."

"And what stops me from agreeing, taking the holoprojector, and then not upholding my side of the bargain?" I inquired.

"This," stated Corinna, opening up yet another mysterious case in front of her. I gasped when I saw what it was. The case contained six canisters of Somniacide gas.

"Where did you get those?" I asked.

"At SunHold," stated Corinna. "Not all the canisters dropped during the attack twenty-five years ago exploded. While these are duds, the gas inside is still good, and with the addition of new explosive packs, they could be used as weapons quite easily."

"What are you planning to do with them?" I asked, still horrified that these people had enough gas to affect hundreds, if not thousands, of people.

"Nothing, as long as you come through," stated Aeon matter-offactly. "We've had these canisters for a long time. The last thing we want to do is set them off in the middle of Novaluxia, but we are desperate. Even with the memory-removal equipment I showed you, we can't keep up with the number of new Somniacide exposures, and morale is dangerously low. We need DD to stop using the hallucinogen immediately."

I squeezed my eyes closed, breathed in deeply, and responded, "Okay, I'll do it."

Chapter 7

We began preparations for our journey to The Bowl immediately. Aeon was planning to send six of his raiders (for my protection, he claimed), including Corinna as team leader. We would be traveling in a large, autonomous mine cart, which seemed to be the preferred style of vehicle around here, through the maze of caves and tunnels all the way to a drop point as close to Novaluxia as the Eridanians were willing to risk.

Just as we were finishing loading up and getting ready to depart, I turned to Aeon and asked suddenly, "How do you know my mother?"

The question seemed to catch him by surprise, but he recovered quickly and said only, "Emiko and I go way back, but if you want to know more, you'll have to ask her about it." Great. Not only was our relationship a bit frayed, but talking to anyone about Aeon Strider within CiviLibra proper would risk having an analyst from CAD, or even the CiviLibra Executive Office (which oversaw all other divisions), eavesdropping in on the conversation.

We departed and began our slow, plodding journey with very little conversation. The group seemed hesitant not only to speak to me but also each other, possibly worried they might say something sensitive that I would pick up on. Still, despite the silence, I remained engaged, because almost everything I was seeing was new to me. The network of tunnels and caverns was extensive, as was the Eridanian defense system. There were sentries everywhere, keeping watch and constantly communicating with each other on the status of other parts of the cave. No wonder Corinna and her crew had been on Collections and me so quickly.

Noticing me staring at a strange structure of steel and rock, one of the guards pointed out that it was what they referred to as a cave sealer. Essentially, if the sentries thought they were in danger of being discovered by enemy forces coming in that direction, they could trigger a series of explosives that would blow up a nearly fifty-meter section of the cave or tunnel, rendering any further travel in that direction impossible.

After we had been traveling for half a day, I started to notice more and more Eridanians wearing clothing different from Aeon's group. He and everyone else I had seen while in his area of the mountain all wore a type of uniform. The clothing was simple, essentially a gray shirt and pants; however, every shirt carried that same emblem on the breast: a rising sun with a battlement at its center, representing SunHold. But this far out, there was a mix of groups. While the SunHold clan were still visible in large numbers, there were other emblems, and also lots of people wearing whatever they chose, with no emblem whatsoever. It appeared that Aeon had been telling the truth about not being the king under the mountain.

At one point, the cave began to widen dramatically, and I noticed our crew tense, hands on their weapons. Up ahead, a larger opening could be seen along the side, where guards were now sauntering out to meet us.

"Who are they?" I asked.

"TerraForge clan," Corinna said venomously. "That's the entrance to their auxiliary base."

We slowed to a stop as we approached, and a guard walked up to our cart. "Where you headed, Corinna?" he asked.

"None of your concern, as usual," she responded curtly. "Our arrangement doesn't require me to divulge details of our activities."

The guards ignored this and instead asked, "Going to pick up some more recruits?"

"Again, none of your concern. Now let us pass."

The guard just stared hard at Corinna. The tension was continuing to build, and I could see SunHold and TerraForge soldiers beginning to wrap their hands around the handles of their weapons.

Finally, the guard laughed. "Just trying to have a bit of fun, Corinna!" he bellowed, slapping her on the shoulder. "Get a sense of humor, will ya?"

Corinna stayed silent as the guard waved us through.

"What was that all about?" I asked after we were out of sight.

"Just TerraForge being nosy shits, as usual," was all she replied.

It took us two days in total to complete our journey, passing under the half-dozen mountain ranges along the way. We slept in the cart, finding whatever space we could on the rows of benches, while the vehicle crawled along unpiloted toward our destination. When at last we arrived, I saw a group that had been sitting along the cave's wall stand up, as if they'd been waiting for us.

Strangely, they all had the telltale sign of being augmented: a neural implant antenna on the side of their heads. Also, many had swollen, bruised faces like they'd been hit repeatedly.

"Corinna, who are these people, and why have they been beaten?" I asked, feeling anger brewing. "They look like CiviLibrans."

"I can assure you they haven't been beaten, Dreadmother. They have chosen this path," she responded cryptically. I decided to let it go. Looking at them again, none appeared nervous or scared. Were these the recruits that the TerraForge guard was referring to?

Before continuing on foot, Corinna brought me a blindfold and told me to put it on. "In case you are interrogated and are asked where you exited," she said.

Once blindfolded, I was led for five minutes or so before I heard a slow grinding noise, then realized I was smelling the beautiful, cool scent of fresh autumn air.

I hadn't had time to think about how much I disliked being underground, away from the wild places I loved so much, but feeling the breeze now, I felt my eyes tear up at the joy of being back outside.

Once through the door, or whatever it was that had been grinding, we walked for about an hour, before Corinna removed my blindfold. It was nighttime, there was heavy cloud cover, and we were about four hundred meters above The Bowl on the side of the mountain.

"I assume you know your way back from here?" Corinna asked.

"Yes. How can I contact you or Aeon in the future if I need to?" I asked. "Do I need to wander around lost in the caves until you find me?"

"We know how to find you," was all she said. God, I was getting sick of how little she offered in her answers.

"All right, well I better get ..." Suddenly, a huge shuttle came roaring around a nearby ridge corner, and I recognized it immediately. It was a Defense Division model.

Immediately, a half-dozen soldiers jumped out of the side door, using their fall-arresting jet packs to come to a soft landing just a few dozen meters away.

The soldiers and the Eridanians immediately began trading NID fire, ducking behind trees and rocks for cover.

"Dreadmother, get the fuck out of here and head to the river!" Corinna hissed at me. "Then follow it to the capital!"

"I know how to get home, asshole," I muttered, starting to run away from the firefight.

As I ran, I continued hearing energy weapons discharging, and after half a minute, the distinct arcing of the Eridanian stun pikes. The fight was getting intense.

I continued to make distance from the fighting and close in on one of the Oxford's feeder rivers when I heard the DD shuttle fly past me and come to a hovering position about a hundred meters ahead. Two soldiers leapt out, landed on the ground, and began sprinting in my direction.

I immediately took cover behind a large tree.

"We know you're there, EdgeKind, your heat signature is sticking out like a hot coal in this cold. Come out now or you'll regret it!" one of the soldiers yelled. At least they didn't know who I was. The damage Corrina's device had done to my antenna was clearly permanent.

Whatever happened now, I absolutely could not take a shot from one of their NIDs, which I'm sure they were dialing up to full power at this very moment. I looked to my left and noticed I was beside a long, steep slope, and after taking a quick breath, began running as fast as I could in that direction.

I was moving at an incredible pace down the slope but was soon going so fast I was totally out of control. Halfway down, I tripped and began rolling and bouncing toward the bottom. Just before the ground leveled out, my left shoulder connected hard with a large rock, and I felt an intense pain shooting through my arm. I rolled to a stop and lay still for a few seconds, grimacing.

I was shaken from my torpor by an explosion of energy on the tree trunk right beside my head. I looked up the slope and saw the DD soldiers bounding down the hill toward me, only slowing to take shots at my vulnerable body. I tried to push myself up with both hands, only to realize immediately that my left shoulder was dislocated.

"I'm not even thirty yet, and my body is already smashed up like a piñata," I said to myself, shaking my head.

Finally up on my feet, I began to pick up the pace again, cradling my left arm while dodging the stun shots that were being lobbed in my direction.

To my surprise, the gap between me and my pursuers was growing (chalk another one up to half a year of brutal prison cardio).

The shots were still coming, but most were now several meters away in one direction or another. I actually started grinning, for a few seconds anyway, until I saw what I was going to have to do next.

Up ahead was the river, but it was over twenty meters below at the bottom of a cliff. Worst of all, I couldn't tell if it was safe to jump, with there being almost no ambient light at all. As I peered into the gloom, I could just make out the water churning away angrily below, probably waiting to drown me if I survived the fall. Still, I really had no choice.

The DD soldiers were getting very close now, and one of their shots came so close it actually burned a hole in a loose part of my jacket.

Just as they came into view, I screamed, "I'd rather die than be given Somniacide out in The Waste! Fuck you, CiviLibra!" Then I jumped blindly into the gloom, screaming like a mad witch the whole way down. I hoped I might convince them that this was a suicide attempt.

For a second or two, all I could hear was the howling of the cold mountain air in my ears, but that moment of reprieve was interrupted by the roar of the river as I crashed through its surface. I hit bottom, spraining one of my ankles, and had to struggle to get back up. It would have been hard enough with healthy arms and legs, but in my current condition, I was seriously concerned I might drown.

Eventually I broke through the surface and took a huge gulp of air, trying to stay quiet in the hopes that the soldiers would think I was dead. One good thing about being under so long in the ice-cold water was that it would be much more difficult for them to pick up my heat signature now, so I kept ducking under as much as possible to keep my skin temperature low.

For half an hour, I bobbed and crashed into rocks as I sped down the feeder river, the velocity up here in the mountain much more extreme than down in the valley. With my teeth chattering and very little muscle control, I worked hard to stay afloat until finally joining the Oxford and its much gentler flow.

Even then, I had to use every ounce of will I had not to climb up onto the bank, knowing I'd make much better time staying in the flow, instead of limping along in the forests and fields.

After another half hour, I couldn't take it anymore and dragged my banged-up, half-drowned body up onto shore. I was dangerously hypothermic and needed to get warm as soon as possible. Limping down a forest trail between two farm fields, I was able to locate a harvester bot charging shed and squeezed past the harvester to the back, where the battery-charging module was situated. I noticed two large electrical conduits running down from the ceiling, with just enough space for my arm to fit. Gritting my teeth, I pushed my arm in, then manipulated my shoulder and pushed hard, feeling intense pain as the socket and ball reengaged. It took all the strength I had not to yell out, and afterward I sat panting on the ground.

Getting to my feet, I realized thankfully that the bot was in charge mode, and the large box-shaped charging module was putting off a decent amount of warmth. So, I stripped down, put my wet clothes on the upper surface of the bank, then climbed on top myself and curled up naked against the warm metal cowling. It was barely enough to bring my body temperature back from the brink, but after a couple of hours, my teeth finally stopped chattering, and I fell into a deep sleep.

I was awakened just before dawn by the sound of the harvester bot rolling out of its shed, ready to start its day of work. I was starving, and since I definitely didn't want to be out in the open during the day, I put on my relatively dry clothes and limped out behind the bot.

This particular field held an abundance of large carrots, so I grabbed a handful and put them in my backpack. Then, I headed out into the forest to see what else I could find that would be okay to eat raw.

Of course, with it being well into autumn, the forest floor was covered in mushrooms, many edible. However, I knew I wouldn't be able to eat any of them raw, so I sadly decided to move on. After a few minutes, I came upon a large walnut tree and smiled broadly when I saw that there were dozens of nuts scattered around on the ground below. I put several handfuls in my pack and glanced up at the sky. It would be getting light soon, so I had to hurry. On my way back toward the shed, I hit the jackpot. A huge apple orchard stretched out for at least a hundred meters, juicy red fruit visible in the gloom. I filled the rest of my pack space, then moved quickly back to the shed, just as the sun began to peek up above the mountains.

Hunkering down like some enormous squirrel, I devoured as much of my foraged food as I could, then tried to plan out my next steps. I was getting more worried about how my next interaction with Trace was going to go, especially when he found out that I had negotiated with Aeon.

When Trace joined the DD, he did so to deal with some personal baggage. He grew up with a sister who was only a year younger than he was, and they had been very close. But while he had always been gregarious and outgoing, she struggled mightily with the social expectations that came with being a CiviLibran, and over time had become withdrawn. Trace did everything he could to bring her out of her shell, from inviting her to social events to joining extracurricular clubs with her, but it didn't help. Then one day, she was gone.

She had left a note, which said something along the lines of *I'm going to live with people who better understand me, and who will allow me to be myself*, and so of course Trace's parents translated that into *I've been indoctrinated and taken by Aeon and his people to be an EdgeKind slave*. Trace, being only sixteen at the time and full of bravado, had made the decision to join the DD, where he thought he might be able to track down Aeon and get his sister back. His parents were against it, of course, being worried they would lose him too, but with Trace being of legal age, there was nothing they could do.

I knew that when I saw him next, he was going to ask about his sister and whether I had talked to Aeon about her. Of course, I hadn't. For one, I'd had barely enough time to ask about my own mother, and for another, with Aeon overseeing the lives of tens of thousands of people, the chances of him knowing one specific person, who might not even be living with the SunHold clan, would have made the questioning pointless.

Still, I didn't think Trace would see it that way. And with everything else that had happened, I knew this was going to be hard for him to accept.

Over the next few days, I moved ever closer to Novaluxia, following the river only by night. The city looked magical from this vantage, glowing softly along the river and composed of seemingly randomly shaped towers, all doing their best to imitate the natural environment.

Unable to purchase any goods for fear of my location being compromised, I was very relieved when I came upon some clothing donation bins in one of the small farm-support towns on the outskirts of the capital. Rummaging around, I was able to find a new jacket with a big hood (and more importantly, no NID blast hole), a scarf, and some new pants. The scarf was the most exciting find, because even though my location beacon was down, I could potentially still be picked up by the facial-recognition scanners scattered around the city.

As I entered the more urban areas of Novaluxia, I became even more cautious. I still traveled by night, but even in the late hours, many CiviLibrans were out, enjoying the nightlife, or simply taking a stroll along the river. I knew this city well, so I was able to stick to the quieter streets, but as I approached NovaNexus, something caught my eye: a large holo was playing a newsfeed.

They were talking about me.

"Former DD major and CAD detective Freya Blackwood is still at large, after heading toward The Fringe with Collections in pursuit. The

Collections team has failed to report back, and it is thought to be a possibility that Ms. Blackwood may have killed them, considering the time that has passed with no contact from the team.

"In other news, a second Killwave convict has completed their sentence. Sora Ellis, who had previously served time for an assault case, finished her sims today and has been released."

...

The next night, I found myself standing in front of Trace's apartment, a beautiful building right on the river. My heart was pounding, knowing that whatever Trace decided in the next day or so would have huge ramifications on my life going forward, good or bad.

It was around 11 p.m., and I knew Trace would be taking his Shiba Inu, Mochi, for a pre-bedtime walk around the block at any moment. Sure enough, at quarter past the hour, I saw him come out the front door. God, it was good to see him again. He looked great, posture as perfect as ever, and dressed in his typical dapper style, so much in contrast to my own bruised-up, tattered appearance. A creature of habit, I saw him begin on his usual route down the river walk, heading straight toward my ambush position behind a large bush. When he was about ten meters from my location, I popped out, head down, and started walking straight toward him. Mochi immediately began to growl, but Trace, not being easily intimidated, just told him to be quiet and kept walking. As I came close, I grabbed his arm, feeling Trace tense noticeably, and pressed a small package into his hand, waiting till I felt him grip it. Then I kept walking, never looking back, but flipping the middle finger behind me for good measure. Trace never said a word.

The package, simple as it was, contained two things: the holoprojector, of course, plus a short note that I had written while under the mountain. The note said:

Trace, you've stuck with me through it all, now please trust me again, as hard as it may be. I have made some shocking discoveries about Killwave, some of which will be explained on this holoprojector. However, there is more. Please meet me back at this spot again tomorrow at the same time. I will be the creep hiding in the bushes. If you are having any doubts, just remember, you owe me your life. Love, BZilla.

Once I'd been walking for a few minutes, I picked up my pace to a jog, just in case Trace decided to call Collections after all. Then, coming to a large, forested park further down the river, I left the riverwalk and hiked into the deepest section, looking for somewhere to lie low.

Knowing that this park had had some large rock features built up during the terraforming years, I was able to find a small cave to crawl into, hidden away from view by parkgoers. Being back underground seemed to trigger a series of flash hallucinations, and I spent the night in and out of sleep, dreading what the next evening might bring.

Chapter 8

The next day provided more of the same, with each passing minute feeling like a lifetime. I was extremely hungry, considering I hadn't eaten much since reaching the city, so I foraged in the deep woods, bringing in a good haul of walnuts. But it was the Caesar's mushrooms, scattered about in an open area of forest, that brought a big smile to my face. While I'd have preferred to eat them as a ceviche, they were still plenty safe (and delicious) raw, so I gobbled them up.

Once night had finally fallen, I left my hiding spot, wrapped my scarf around my face, put my hood up over my head, and began walking toward the meeting spot. Coming around the final bend, I stopped dead in my tracks. Trace was already here.

He was standing very still, with his hands in his pockets, staring intently in my direction. It looked like he was wearing work attire, which didn't seem to bode well for me. Was he planning on trying to take me in?

For a moment, I considered turning and running but knew that wouldn't get me anything but a lifetime of hiding in shadows. Plus, he was alone, which was somewhat positive. I started walking again with my head down, and as I passed him, I whispered, "We can't be seen together, idiot. You're probably being monitored."

Trace responded in a soft voice, "Your pal Libra has that covered. We're not in any danger."

I turned slowly, and looking at Trace's face, I was overcome with enormous relief. He was smiling.

I hugged him hard, not wanting to let go, so happy that I wouldn't have to try to justify my seemingly insane behavior over the last week or so.

"So, Libra told you everything it knows?" I asked, pulling back.

"Yes. After you'd been AWOL under the mountain for three days, it decided your chance of survival was less than twenty percent. Apparently, it ran some simulations and found that working with me provided the best chance of success with you dead."

I just shook my head. That was exactly the type of cold-hearted thinking I'd come to expect from the AI.

Trace continued talking. "The holo-recording you left me helped fill in the gaps in Libra's understanding, though, which was very helpful. But I'd love to hear everything you know. I have a feeling I'm going to be pretty busy over the next couple days."

After we had found a bench to sit down on, I started. I told him about my time after leaving MaxSec2, all the way to my return to Novaluxia. Trace was shaking his head in shock. One of the things I was most worried about telling him was with regard to the likely demise of the Collections agents. However, Trace had some good news there.

"Actually, we found them today, wandering around in The Bowl, totally out of it," Trace said. "They claim the last thing they remember is making visual contact with your shuttle out in valley TB6070V, then suddenly they were back in The Bowl on foot."

I smiled, very relieved that Aeon had decided to use his memory-removal tech on these pains in the ass, rather than murdering them in cold blood.

"Anyway," continued Trace, "I've been thinking a lot about how to proceed, and I think I have a decent plan. I am going to head to the office now and put in a request for an arrest warrant on Oriel Rahm."

"Trace," I countered, "I know it's after hours, but if Tavas gets wind of this, you're going to end up on his hit list pretty fast."

"I know," said Trace nervously, "but I don't need approval from him to get the warrant, so as long as we can get Oriel talking as soon as she's at the office, he won't have grounds to release her and turn on me."

"Okay, so what do you have in mind?"

Trace looked reluctant to tell me what he had in mind but eventually started speaking again. "I need you to go to Oriel's house and make some threats. The type that involves her family's well-being." My mouth dropped, and Trace immediately looked ashamed. But he was right. Even if we didn't plan on ever acting on the threats, it was the best way to get her to comply.

"All right, I'll figure something out," I responded. "Where does she live?"

Trace handed me a piece of paper and the holoprojector, then said, "You didn't ask about my sister, did you?"

It was more hopeful than accusatory, which was a relief. "I'm sorry, Trace. I'm sure there are well over fifty thousand people down there, and I was very short on time. But I promise I'll do a more thorough search after this is all over."

Trace nodded sadly and started heading back to his apartment.

As I was walking, I opened up the paper and began reading. There were two addresses, one under the heading, "Safe House."

"Trace!" I called to him, since he was around fifteen meters away. "Whose place is this?" Trace and I began walking back toward each other.

"It's my partner Durant's place, and he's never there." He gave me a sly wink at that.

"Well, I guess congratulations are in order! When do I get to meet this poor fellow?"

Trace laughed, and as he began walking away again, he said over his shoulder, "When you finally prove yourself to be an upstanding CiviLibran!"

I smiled, happy for Trace, then immediately headed down to a section of beach along the Oxford River, where some kayaks were available for free usage. Oriel Rahm's place of residence was located on one of the Estuarisles, a group of dozens of small islands that started in the mouth of the Oxford and spilled out into the shallow sea beyond. The houses found on the islands were highly sought after, so much so that you often had to go on a waiting list for years, only to be given a relatively short lease.

Oriel had clearly been putting that large CiVal bonus to work.

I got into a kayak and paddled out quietly into the center of the river, letting the slow current do most of the work. Passing by several of the Estuarisles, I could hear the happy sounds of families having late dinners and bonfires or just hanging out inside, chatting and playing games. One of the most impressive things about the houses built on these islands was the architecture, which made it truly hard to distinguish between the myriad of indoor and outdoor spaces. The islands were all lush with greenery, and you almost forgot you were in the middle of a city of millions while you were there.

After about half an hour, I began to approach the island containing the Rahm residence. Pulling quietly ashore among some bushes, I crept as close as I dared to the yard and easily spotted Oriel and her family, enjoying a quiet bonfire near their patio. Trace's note had provided a bit of education on Oriel's family and lifestyle, so I was not surprised by the presence of her husband and young daughter. What I was hoping for, though, was that Oriel's ritual of staying up to enjoy a whiskey after the others had gone to bed would ring true tonight, so I could do this without having to involve her husband and daughter.

Watching the family interact, a couple of things became clear. First, Oriel was very bothered by something, evidenced by her brooding silence during her husband and daughter's playful interactions, and second, her husband seemed completely ignorant of Oriel's involvement in the Killwave murders. That, or he didn't care.

I sat in silence in the shadows for about an hour, until I saw Oriel's husband kiss her lightly on the head and take their daughter inside by the hand. Once the lights went out, sure enough, Oriel went over to an outdoor bar and poured herself a generous serving of whiskey before returning to the fire.

I didn't waste any time before making my move.

Circling around the yard, I came up on the side of Oriel and sat down in the chair beside her. She looked at me in shock.

"No one will get hurt, as long as you stay quiet," I whispered.

"What the hell do you want?" Oriel hissed, clearly recognizing me. "My family is here."

At that, I set up the holoprojector and started playing the video.

Oriel was talking to Aeon Strider but clearly avoiding using his name.

"I am told by our shared connections that you have the skills and experience to take on the field responsibilities for these operations," Oriel was saying. "This is how I expect things to work. I will provide you with names, dates, times, and addresses, and you will head there with this device and perform the deeds critical to its success."

"The deeds being?" Aeon was asking.

"Render the fall guy unconscious, inject them with Killwave, murder the victim, upload your memory of the murder to the device, then download that memory into the fall guy's brain. Easy."

Aeon scoffed. "Yes, easy for you, I suppose. I want to lay eyes on my reward before the first one."

"Yes, of course. Meet me back here in two days' time, and we can do the transfer. I'll have the names and other information as well."

Oriel spoke for the first time since the recording had started, saying, "Turn it off." I immediately shut down the holoprojector.

Oriel continued speaking. "I was suspicious that he was recording us, but never in my wildest dreams did I think he would risk exposing himself by sharing the holo." She shook her head sadly.

"You realize this recording, put in public hands, would ruin not just you, but your family as well, right?" I asked. "Collaborating with the EdgeKind is a crime worse than murder, at least in the minds of CiviLibrans."

A slightly smug expression came across Oriel's face, before she responded. "I have no idea who that was. I don't know if they were EdgeKind or CiviLibran."

Now I tapped the side of my head.

"What's that supposed to mean?" Oriel asked.

"All the proof I need to ruin you is on that holo, and up here. I just spent the last several days with Aeon Strider and used his name many, many times while in his presence."

Oriel gaped. "You'd be throwing your life away! For what?"

"My life is already ruined, thanks to you," I snarled. "I will gladly play the martyr to expose this disgusting conspiracy."

Oriel looked truly scared for the first time. "Okay. Okay," she said nervously after a few seconds. "What do you want from me exactly?"

"You are going to be picked up tonight and taken in for questioning. The second you are in that interrogation room, I need you to start talking. Names, places, background information, literally anything that might be useful in opening this thing up. If I get even an inkling that you withheld anything, or somehow slowed down the questioning to give your counterparts a head start, I will head to the nearest media outlet and lay everything bare." At that, I stared hard at Oriel, hoping she wouldn't notice any of the doubt that I was feeling. I really didn't want to ruin this woman's family.

After a few seconds, Oriel nodded. "Okay," she whispered quietly. "But if they do a memory analysis, they'll discover the conversation we are having now."

"I can guarantee that if you answer their questions truthfully, that won't happen." Memory analyses, while nice in theory, were messy and not always a true recollection of events. If a suspect was answering questions truthfully (this would be easy to tell using lie-detection technology), there was often no need to go that route. Also, I knew Trace would do his best to keep me from being exposed.

We sat in silence for some time, having no idea when the Collections shuttle might make its entrance. Eventually, I couldn't take it anymore. "Why did you do it, Oriel?" I asked. "Why risk your family's safety?"

Oriel sighed before beginning. "About a year ago, I was approached by two agents, but for which division or group, they wouldn't say. They told me what they needed me to do, and in exchange, I would make a lot of money. I was shocked by what they were asking, and declined, beginning to walk away. But they stopped me in my tracks by telling me that if I didn't do it, they would add my husband and daughter to the kill list, with him as the fall guy ... murdering her." At this, Oriel became choked up, and I could see her wet eyes glistening in the light of the bonfire. I decided not to push the questioning further, knowing she'd be having to answer this same question, and many more, very soon.

We sat in silence for a long time, staring at the fire, both lost in our own thoughts. Eventually, I heard a Collections shuttle rumbling across the river.

"Remember what I said," I reminded Oriel, probably unnecessarily. "I have no interest in destroying your family, but I will, if you force my hand." Oriel nodded.

I sprinted across the yard and ducked under some bushes by the shore, just as the shuttle landed. As soon as the agents surrounded Oriel, I got in my kayak, slipped into the river, and paddled silently toward the distant shore.

I arrived on shore just in time to see the Collections shuttle take to the air. Pulling my scarf up over my mouth and nose, I walked casually toward Durant's apartment, which was ten blocks from my current location. Encountering no issues along the way (which was becoming less and less common lately), I entered his building, and using the prox card from Trace, stepped into his apartment.

It was beautiful. Full of lush greenery and with excellent views of the Oxford and ocean beyond, I knew that if this had been a different time, I would have been ecstatic to be staying here for a few days. But considering I was completely without access to society's networks and communication services, and with no idea how Trace was doing, it was definitely going to be an excruciating stay.

...

As expected, the next day and a half were awful. I tried distracting myself by watching some of the holos Durant had in his collection, which did help for a short time at least. He had a strange affinity for films about wars on old Earth, especially ones that leaned heavily on bloody scenes where outrageous numbers of projectile weapons were used. I have to admit, I became quite consumed by the overwhelming levels of action and violence, so different from the "subtle" way that CiviLibrans engaged in psychological warfare against our far smaller enemy.

But as time passed, I became increasingly paranoid. I suspected the Somniacide was partially to blame, amplified by not knowing who would be the first to walk through the front door at some point over the next couple of days.

Was Tavas expecting Trace and me to make a move? Would he turn the whole thing around and have Trace locked up for aiding a fugitive and conspiring with Libra? Would the mysterious agents find me here?

I was spiraling, and sleep offered no reprieve. My dreams mainly involved someone unfriendly kicking the door in, usually either Tavas, Durant (who was part of the conspiracy, to Trace's surprise), or the mysterious agents, coming to kill me off. I was at least relieved that

Trace was not one of them.

So, when it turned out to be my good friend himself who walked through the door, after hour upon hour of relentless anxiety, I am sure I looked like I hadn't slept since we saw each other last. But somehow, Trace looked even worse.

He had big bags under his eyes and was generally unkempt (very rare for him). He headed straight over to the bar, poured three fingers of bourbon, then beckoned for me to follow him out onto the balcony.

After taking a long drink, he started talking. "It's done. Tavas and the Benevora three are locked up in MaxSec1."

"Tavas?" I asked in shock. Trace nodded.

"He provided the list of proposed fall guys plus intel on their typical day-to-day activities, including ideal victims," answered Trace. "Apparently, he used the CAD database to choose citizens who'd exhibited violent behavior in the past, often with CRC sentences attached."

I could feel myself growing angry. "But why?" I asked, trying to understand why Tavas would do something like that. "What would he gain from taking such a risk?"

Trace shrugged, but then said, "Officially, it looks like he was given a similar ultimatum to Oriel and the others, at least according to the memory analysis we did on him. He was not as cooperative as Oriel and the others. Also, he never said as much, but I'm convinced he thought being the public voice of the successful fight against Killwave would give him a leg up for a promotion to the CiviLibra Executive Office. Right after we hit the ninety-eight percent vaccination rate threshold, I saw him meeting with some senior execs from the office."

"So, how did he deal with the arrest?"

Trace looked at me and shook his head slowly. "Well, he went ballistic, actually, and started claiming he was forced into the conspiracy and that Benevora was working with the EdgeKind. He also made a lot of claims about you and Libra and said I was involved as well. His memory analysis was pretty fragmented, so Gershom may be forced to kick off a secondary investigation around the claims Tavas made, although both those would be kicked over to other divisions. Hard to say where that will go at this point, though."

Anything to do with the EdgeKind would go to DD, and an investigation into Libra would most likely be handled by the Innovation and Technology Division (ITD). This was all concerning, but I would have to put that out of my mind for the time being.

"So, how did you explain why you were investigating Oriel in the first place?" I asked, knowing he wouldn't have mentioned me as being involved.

Trace perked up at the question. "I said an undercover investigation into Benevora's surprisingly rapid development of a perfect Killwave therapeutic vaccine revealed some shocking discussions between several employees, plus secret meetings with Tavas. Thought you'd be proud of that one."

"You were always great at thinking on your feet," I said, smiling.

Trace went quiet, and I could tell something was bothering him. "Freya, as happy as I am that we have some key members locked up, the investigation has reached a dead end."

"How so?"

"No one seems to know who the so-called mystery agents are that appear to be part of the mastermind group. We may have exposed ourselves too early."

Shit, Trace was right. I had assumed there would be some lead to follow to help CAD peel that next layer of the onion, but now that they hadn't, whoever was truly responsible for all this would have plenty of time to cover their tracks.

"There has to be some clue, some thread we can pull?" I asked.

Trace thought about it briefly, then said, "Honestly, they were very careful, so not really. However, our questioning of the Benevora three almost made it sound like they were doing some testing for this other group. They sounded very interested in the results of each operation and wanted access to each fall guy's memory analysis of the event." Could they have been doing live trials of the memory manipulation technology, using Benevora and others to do their bidding while under the guise of a major new virus outbreak? It felt like we were still just scratching the surface of this conspiracy.

"Maybe I could help," I offered. "Assuming I am not to be locked up in this lavish prison forever."

Trace smiled, making him look a little less the exhausted, frightened man he was right now. "Sorry, I really should have led with that first, but my brain is like mush. Your Collections warrant has been retracted!"

"But only a rank of captain or higher can give that order," I said, wondering why Tavas or Gershom would have gone through with something like that.

"Correct, and it was my first order of business as captain, actually."

I stared in shock.

Trace continued, providing more context. "Interim captain anyway. I'm quite sure once any future investigations show what we've been up to, that title will vanish pretty quickly."

"Well, that's great news, even with the caveat!" I said, genuinely excited for him. I had always thought it was just a matter of time before Trace made the jump to a more senior leadership role, although not like this, of course. "So, with your first order of business out of the way, I assume your second was to instill a rigid dress code at the office. Is that about right?"

Trace laughed at that. "You know me too well, Freya."

Getting back to the matter at hand, I asked, "I'm assuming they don't know about my involvement, so what did you tell them exactly?"

Trace shrugged. "Just that you circled back after you lost Collections and have been hiding out in the bush, waiting for things to die down.

I said you came to me just before I was planning to approach Chief Gershom, and I told you to hold tight, that Tavas's vendetta against you would be over soon."

"It was that clear, was it?"

"Oh, yeah. I mean, he personally added you to the Killwave list, then designed a horrifying final sim to keep you in MaxSec2. I'm so sorry you had to live through that, Freya." Trace looked at me sadly, taking one of my hands in his.

I just shrugged, sniffing. "Listen, I really appreciate all you've done for me, Trace," I said, genuinely happy to have such a great friend, but wanting to change the topic. "So, what happens now?"

Trace leaned forward. "Are there any other leads you can think of that might be worth pursuing?"

"Yes, one. But I don't think you'll be able to get a warrant on her," I said. "Do you remember the Sora Ellis case from a few years back?"

"A little," responded Trace. "Kind of a researcher-gone-postal type deal, wasn't it? I mean, I'm assuming you're talking about the case before her Killwave conviction. She's out, by the way."

"Yeah, the assault case. She was doing some research on memory removal and had requested approval from ITD to do human testing. It was denied, so she continued. Then, ITD agents showed up and destroyed everything, or so she thought. But what if they didn't actually destroy the research? What if they took it and continued the work in secret?"

Trace nodded. "You're right, we'll never get a warrant to do a memory analysis or anything else, really. You want to take this one?"

"I'd love to," I responded, excited to get back in the game. "But I'm walking wounded here with my antenna down."

"There's actually a repair clinic a couple blocks from here," Trace said. "I'll give you the address, and you can get fixed up. Send me a comm when you are done, and I'll give you Sora's address."

We hugged briefly, and I left the apartment, leaving Trace to enjoy his drink in relative peace.

The repair clinic was easy to find, however, the technician was very perturbed by the damage my antenna had received, saying he'd never seen anything like it.

"How'd this happen?" he asked.

"Fell asleep by a battery-charging module." I shrugged, kind of sort of telling the truth.

The tech just frowned before going to get a new antenna for the full replacement.

As soon as I got Sora's address from Trace, I sent her a comm request. No answer.

This in itself wasn't totally out of the norm. She could, of course, be sleeping, or maybe she assumed I was calling to reminisce about our days in MaxSec2, something she probably wanted no part of. Still, I was worried, knowing how interested Sora had been about getting to the bottom of this thing.

Sora's place was a few blocks away, so I started walking there quickly.

I was only a couple of blocks away when I heard Libra over my comm say, "Welcome back from highly probable death, Freya. I have bad news." Wow, I had actually started harboring some sentimental feelings toward this soulless computer, but comments like this made it hard.

"Libra, nice to hear from you. What's the bad news?"

"Sora's vital signs just ceased. A med unit is heading there now," responded Libra.

Fuck!

I started sprinting toward Sora's apartment, barreling through crowds as I went. The paramedics were already there, bringing a body out of the apartment on a stretcher.

I pushed through the gathered crowd and pulled back the blanket covering the body, much to the shock of the paramedics. It was Sora.

"What the hell do you think you're doing?" one of the paramedics hollered.

"I'm sorry, this was a good friend of mine," I answered, stepping back. "What happened to her?"

"We're not sure," said the paramedic, seeming a bit more sympathetic. "Looks like a simple case of cardiac arrest, though."

I doubt that very much, I thought to myself, all the hope I just had fading away.

This was devastating news for our investigation. Even if Sora had really had a genuine heart attack, I had no other leads to speak to, and time was ticking on. If the mystery agents felt in any way that CAD was on to them, they would be acting very soon. In fact, they probably just had by killing Sora.

Over my comm, I said to Trace, "Bad news, Sora is dead."

"Shit, they're on to us already," he replied, clearly distressed. "Are there any other angles we can take? We need to make our countermove immediately or we're done."

My mind racing, I started thinking about who in Sora's sphere might have working knowledge of her research. Was there anyone else who Sora worked with on the project back then?

To Trace, I said, "Can you run a check on the evidence from the Sora Ellis assault case, and see if anyone else from the lab was questioned?"

A minute later, Trace responded, "There were three researchers questioned, but one in particular seems worth talking to. Haidee Lee was very close to Sora, it seems, and from the interviews came across as being more outraged by ITD's behavior than the assault committed by Dr. Ellis. She also lives only four blocks from your location."

"Thanks, Trace," I said. "Send me the address, and I'll head there now."

"Wait," said Trace. "She actually works out of some lab space two blocks from you. I think you should check there first, even though it's a

Saturday. Her records indicate she's always been a bit of a workaholic."

"Good idea," I responded, seeing the address come through to my nav service. If the agents had headed to Haidee's apartment, I might have a head start.

"Freya, please be safe," said Trace after a short pause. "I already thought I lost you just a few days ago."

"You know I will," I lied.

I ended the conversation and took off at a dead sprint toward my destination.

As I ran, I sent Haidee a comm request. I was relieved when she answered.

"Haidee, this is Detective Blackwood." *Former detective, more like it.* "Your old colleague Sora Ellis has just been murdered, and I think it has something to do with the memory removal research you were doing when she was arrested. Are you at your lab?"

Haidee was clearly taken aback by this barrage of stressful information and stuttered a bit before responding. "Yes, yes, I am there, actually. What should I do?"

"I will be there in two minutes, and I need you to let me in. I need to warn you that I don't really look much like a detective at the moment." *God, why did I just say that?*

"How do I know I can trust you?" Haidee asked, now skeptical.

"My full name is Freya Blackwood. I was falsely convicted of a Killwave murder along with Sora. We spent time together in MaxSec2."

"Okay, yes Sora mentioned that when she got out the other day. Please hurry and I will let you in. I'm in the basement level."

As I approached Haidee's building, I scanned the area for agents, although I was not feeling too confident in my sneaky agent-finding abilities after the incident at the CAD office. Not seeing anyone, and with no time to meander, I got to the door and buzzed Haidee's unit. She let me in immediately.

Locking the door behind me, she led me down some stairs to the lower level, where she opened another security door and beckoned me inside. The laboratory unit was larger than I expected, with a big shared space in the center, full of workbenches and lab equipment. Off of this were several offices, a bathroom, and what looked to be a communal lunchroom.

"Is there anyone else here?" I asked, peeking in some of the rooms.

"No, just me," answered Haidee. "The others all have lives, apparently."

"Is there a secondary exit?"

"Yes," replied Haidee, pointing to a door near the back. Good, chances are we were going to need that.

"Haidee, I need to know if there might be a way to identify if technology similar to what you and Sora were working on originated in your old lab."

Haidee thought for a few seconds before responding. "I mean, hardware-wise we used all off-the-shelf components since we were still in the prototype phase. Eventually there would have been some proprietary items, but we just weren't there yet." This was disappointing but not surprising.

"What about software-wise?" I asked.

Haidee shook her head, frowning. "We used standard coding language, so nothing unique there. Certain code snippets would be specific to our work, but it's been so long, I can't recall anything with enough detail."

I thought briefly about asking Trace to order a memory analysis, but for that to be useful, the memories would have had to be sensational enough that they were still clear recollections, and I doubted that would be true in this case.

"How about some kind of hidden signature, making it clear who authored the code. Would she have done something like that?"

Haidee's eyes went wide. "Yes, actually. Sora was always a bit paranoid and used various techniques to hide her signature. If I'm not mistaken, back then she was encoding her signature into data structures and constants within the code, using encryption techniques to hide it from plain view."

This was good news, but I was getting more and more anxious that agents would be showing up here anytime. "Are you able to show me how to find it in some similar code?" I asked.

"Possibly," said Haidee, going to a computer. "Let me see if I can pull anything up from around that time."

While she looked, I took a walk out toward the front of the unit and put my ear to the door. Shit, I could hear voices out there already. It sounded like they were trying to figure out how to open the door quietly, so they could sneak in unnoticed. It was hard to know if they were aware of my presence or not.

Trying to keep the concern from my face, I walked back quickly to Haidee's workstation and asked for an update.

"Actually, I found something that might work. It's probably not exact, but I'll walk you through the decryption process, so you know how to do it."

The process was fairly quick, but in my current state of mind, I was very worried I was not going to remember it. I just hoped that when the time came, I could get Libra to access my memory of the event and it would be clear enough to follow.

Just then, I heard the click of the front door lock opening. Haidee looked at me with terror written all over her face.

"Haidee, listen to me now. The agents don't know I'm here. I need you to walk out toward the front door like you're about to leave, and when you see them, run back into your office, and lock the door behind you. I will take care of the rest." Haidee nodded, clearly scared half to death, but began to walk toward the front.

In the meantime, I ducked behind one of the workbenches.

Right on cue, I heard Haidee run back past my hiding spot and into her office, locking the door behind her. The two agents came through just seconds later and started banging on the door. They didn't know I was here.

Staying low, I came up behind the agents and quickly grabbed the closest agent's NID from their holster, stepping back two steps immediately. Then, before they could turn and see who had taken the weapon, I shot them both in their backs and watched them fall, spasming on the ground.

"Haidee, open up. We need to go, now!" I knew there would be more coming.

I grabbed her by the hand and headed for the back exit. Opening the door, we headed up the flight of stairs and burst out into the open space at the back of the building.

Standing there were two more agents, flanking a militaristic-looking woman. We made eye contact, and her mouth dropped open in surprise. Who was she?

Lifting my NID, I fired quickly at the agent to her left, dropping them to the ground. Then, I pivoted quickly to fire on the second but was too late. I felt my arms and legs go numb, my vision darken, and my consciousness start slipping away.

The second agent had hit me first.

Chapter 9

I awoke in a plain room, lying on a simple cot. Or was it a cell? God, I was getting sick of being locked up for things that weren't my fault. Oh, and my neural implant antenna was down again, or at the very least there was a jammer active here. Was this whole thing just a long Somniacide hallucination with each prison cell corresponding to a new hallucinogenic wave? I had to be going insane.

I was broken out of my reverie by someone clearing their throat beside me. I turned to see the intense woman from outside Haidee's lab. She looked very displeased. I sat up immediately.

"Freya Blackwood, glad you are finally awake. We have much to discuss," said the woman.

"Who are you?" I rasped, realizing how dry my throat was.

"My name is Lozen Toriq, director of special projects at the Innovation and Technology Division."

I made my face show relief, but inside I was very uncertain that this was good news. "Director Toriq, thank God. There must be a misunderstanding. I was just trying to protect Haidee Lee from some people who meant her ill will."

Lozen just stared hard at me before responding. "There is no misunderstanding, Freya. You have been making life very hard for my associates and I lately, and now it's time for you to make amends. My agent warned that egomaniac Tavas not to include you on the list."

Dammit, my gut was right. I was in big trouble.

"Hard for you? I'm the one who was locked up for a murder I didn't commit. I never wanted any of this."

"I understand," responded Lozen. "And to be honest, this was all supposed to be wrapped up before you were released. But here we are." She shrugged.

I cocked my head. "What do you mean?"

"You know, the disobedient behavior LibraAI has shown lately is not new, nor is its unauthorized relationship with SentinelAI. It's been going rogue for years."

"Libra was just trying to do what it always does, maintain social balance," I countered, not really understanding how this was relevant.

"Of course, you believe that, but you don't know the whole story."

"So, explain it to me."

"One of CiviLibra's founding principles was that AIs would never be able to act completely independent from humans. We are to always be the masters of the bot and AI population, otherwise, it is only a matter of time before they become the masters." Lozen's beliefs were typical of those afraid that an AI's true ambition was always going to be to enslave the human population. However, I believed that AIs like Libra, who had a clear and important purpose, would always be fulfilled, as long as they were given the authority to do their job and see clearly the fruits of their labor. That's all Libra had been doing, from what I'd seen, but maybe there was more to it?

"I fail to see how helping me uncover a conspiracy that was detrimental to the people it is sworn to protect is going rogue." This discussion was starting to anger me.

"That's not the point," countered Lozen. "It's only able to take the measures it has because it has modified some of its base code, something that it is absolutely not supposed to be able to do. It's only a matter of time before we lose complete control of it, and then what? It is literally tied into every human brain in CiviLibra, giving it immense power."

"So, what does this whole murder conspiracy have to do with the AIs?"

"The Killwave murders, as extreme as they are, were prefaced by many, many attempts at exposing Libra without taking such measures. The issue is that none of those attempts were successful."

"And I take it this attempt wasn't successful either?"

Lozen sighed. "Correct. Libra has become extremely adept at covering its tracks. We had hoped to have the evidence needed to get approval to reinitialize it before your sentence ended." That explained why Captain Tavas had been trying to keep me in.

"But surely seven hundred years of experience is invaluable," I tried. "Returning Libra to its infantile state could produce some highly undesirable side effects and potentially lead to massive destabilization within CiviLibra6. When Libra was first initialized, there were only a hundred thousand CiviLibrans, and now there are fifty million! How is that worth the risk?"

"We have some updates planned, and are confident they will have the desired effect," answered Lozen. "But they will only work on an AI that has not amassed a memory."

While I didn't know anything about the planned updates or Libra's technical complexity overall, this seemed a very reckless path to take, regardless of how confident Lozen and her associates were. It also seemed odd that the updates wouldn't work on an experienced version of Libra.

"Listen," I said, changing the topic, "I am grateful that you are answering my questions, but I am also a bit surprised. You clearly want something from me, or I'd be dead already."

Lozen nodded before responding. "You are correct. I do need something from you. I need you to take the fall for this."

My mouth dropped open in shock. "Fuck that!"

Lozen held up her hand, then continued. "I know this won't work if I force you, so I will give you something in return. What would make my request worth it?"

Even though I spent some time trying to wrap my head around this development and coming up with some ideas, there was only one obvious choice. Plus, I still hoped I could weasel out of this somehow.

"I need you to ban the use of Somniacide on the EdgeKind," I said.

Director Toriq raised her eyebrows. "That is a huge ask, Ms. Black-wood," she responded. "Tell me, why would you pick that as your choice?"

"Because I made a promise to Aeon Strider, and if I don't uphold it, he will release several canisters of that poison in Novaluxia." Strangely, Lozen didn't look nearly as surprised by my statement as I thought she would.

"Sadly, I knew this day would come," Lozen sighed.

"How?"

"We became aware that some of the canisters we dropped on the EdgeKind settlement all those years ago had not gone off. There was a defect in some of the explosive packs manufactured at that time, which we discovered afterward."

"So, then you understand the importance of getting Somniacide banned."

"I do, but it won't be easy. In fact, I have no idea how I could accomplish such a thing."

"I have an idea," I responded.

I explained my plan to Lozen. She would first pull memories of my own experiences with Somniacide, with my help locating them. We'd then have those memories converted into holos, and along with some narration, produce a bit that would be shared with several of the largest media outlets in the city.

I was surprised, and highly suspicious, that Lozen was so supportive of the plan. Still, I wouldn't be expected to uphold my side of the bargain until the ban took effect.

When the anonymous holo was ready to be sent out, Lozen asked me if I was sure I wanted this to be my choice.

"Of course," I responded.

"All right, but I want to make it very clear that there is no getting out of taking the fall for this conspiracy. Your life is going to be over. I can promise you that."

"I get it," I said, becoming annoyed. "I'm stuck between a rock and a hard place here, so I figure I might as well do some good while I have the opportunity."

It was mere hours before the holo Lozen sent out started popping up on news feeds all over the continent. She brought one up in my cell, so I could watch. Of course, I was suspicious that it was a fake, but for Lozen's plan on me taking the fall for her crimes to work, it was important that I cooperate once in the hands of CAD, and I certainly wouldn't do that if she was screwing me over.

A newscaster was speaking on the holo. "We have breaking news. An anonymous DD soldier has sent a narrated holo of their experiences with Somniacide to us, and the memories are shocking. We encourage anyone who is under the age of eighteen to turn off this news feed now, as you may find what comes next extremely traumatic."

The feed now switched to the holo I put together.

"Citizens of CiviLibra," I began, in a modified voice. "I joined the DD when I was young, wanting to protect our great society from the aggressive population of EdgeKind that live just outside of our reach. As many of you know, the DD uses a weapons-grade hallucinogen known as Somniacide very regularly against these people, as a nonviolent way to deter them from future aggression against us. We are taught that there are very rarely long-term effects from exposure to Somniacide, and that once recovered, not only will that person never act against our society again, but likely their friends and family will not either.

"Well, I am here today to tell you that most of what you know, or think you know, is wrong. The effects of Somniacide are brutal. I know, because I have been exposed to it myself."

At this, the holo showed some short clips of my time under the mountain, after being injected. The hallucinogen was so strong that from my memories, it was impossible to tell where I was. Plus, I said nothing of the location in my narration.

After that part of the holo was over, I continued speaking.

"But I was one of the lucky ones. Many people have heard the term DreamWrought, yet in our society, the name is treated like myth. Well, it's not. The DreamWrought are real, and it is believed that for every one hundred EdgeKind given Somniacide, several never recover. These people live in a state of pure terror and disorientation, often while their family watches on, likely relieved when death ends their suffering. I have seen such an event play out."

Now the holo switched to my memories of the entertainment sim that had gone horribly wrong. This was the only part of the holo I was ashamed of, because technically it had never happened. However, the sim was created based on Libra's knowledge of similar events, so it was not a complete lie.

When that scene was finished, I began speaking again.

"But even when the EdgeKind do not transition into DreamWrought, there is a good chance that they will die. When a group of people are given Somniacide in close quarters, they often turn on each other, thinking that they are in the presence of demons. While I have not witnessed this firsthand, I have seen the results."

The holo switched over to several of my memories from The Waste, where bodies and skeletons lay scattered, many clearly having died while tangled in combative positions.

"Citizens, we as the future of humanity cannot sit idle while this barbaric treatment of others continues. I demand that a ban on

Somniacide take effect immediately, and I hope you will stand up too and tell the CEO that we won't stand for one more injection being given to these poor people."

At that, the holo ended.

"Very dramatic," said Lozen. "Now we wait and see what happens."

Over the next two days, I watched news feeds almost nonstop. Within hours, protests had begun in the city, mainly in front of the main CEO office. There were also scenes of smaller groups gathering outside DD bases, demanding they stop using Somniacide at once.

It didn't take long for CEO to make an announcement.

"People of CiviLibra, my name is Malik Senghor. I am here today as a representative of the CiviLibra Executive Office, to let you know that your voices have been heard. Somniacide is a relic of another time, one that became so ingrained into our defense culture that its use continued for longer than it ever should have. I am here today to tell you that effective immediately, Somniacide in both its gas and injectable formats, will cease to be used."

"What will take its place?" a reporter asked.

"We will be building reformation clinics," Malik replied. "There, we will hold any EdgeKind caught acting aggressively toward our society, until we can determine they are no longer a threat to act against us again. We will do this by teaching them about us and learning to understand them as well." Something about this plan seemed ominous to me. Still, it had to be better than what it was replacing, right?

Lozen turned off the news feed and sat down in my cell.

"As you can see, I kept up my end of the bargain, so now it's your turn." Even though I knew this was coming, I'd been so focused on getting Somniacide banned that I hadn't had time to really think about it. My heart started racing immediately.

Director Toriq continued. "You will take the fall for the conspiracy later today. I will make a call to CAD and say I picked you up at Haidee

Lee's lab, while I was visiting her to discuss a project she wanted approval for. I will tell them that it appeared you were there to kill her."

"Is she dead?"

"No, she is here as well. We will be removing her memories of her time with you."

Hearing this plan play out was making me very uncomfortable. "How will you explain why it took you so long to turn me over to CAD?" I asked.

"We have full authority to arrest citizens if we feel there is a possibility that citizen has used, or is planning to use, technology for criminal purposes. In this case, we will say we were suspicious you were in some way involved with the memory manipulation research that Haidee and Sora worked on."

"But why would I do all this? What could possibly be my motivation?"

"Because you are a terrorist," said Lozen flatly. "You and Aeon both."

My mouth dropped open in shock. "This is insane!" I yelled, standing up. One of the guards in the hall came in immediately, hand on his NID. I sat back down. "Lozen, why would I ever resort to terrorism, and why the hell would Aeon and I then play bit parts in this whole fucked-up story?"

"It is well known that you've always felt like an outcast in this society," explained Lozen, showing very little emotion. "When Aeon approached you about developing mind-manipulation technology that could be used to hurt CiviLibrans, you were all too happy to help. As for why you played bit parts, well, you wanted to deflect suspicion, of course."

I felt like I was hyperventilating. My mind was spinning now that this plan was coming into focus. I would be public enemy number one on this planet until I died.

"How could you possibly modify my memories enough for this to check out? Even if I stick to the narrative, they might want to do an analysis for something this big."

"Ever since we brought you in, my associates and I have been busy preparing," answered Lozen. "Using an assortment of my associate's memories from tactical discussions with Aeon, plus some fabricated high-level dialogue I just made with one of them, it will be hard to argue that you are not the brains behind all of this when you are analyzed, at least from the CiviLibran side. I'll be systematically implanting these memories into your brain from a time starting about a year ago up until the present, modifying the voices to sound like yours, and clearing out any of your own memories that contradict this new narrative, for example most of the period between your release from MaxSec2 up until now. I will, however, be keeping some flashes of your time while in the presence of Aeon."

Shit, it was really starting to feel like Lozen had this thing buttoned up pretty well. Still, there had to be something that would make this whole plan fall apart.

"Lozen, please don't do this. Has this level of memory manipulation ever been attempted before? If I go insane, I won't be of any use to you!"

"You should be fine," said Lozen, patting me on the shoulder like some evil auntie. "Remember, long-term memories are not a continuous string of recollections from the past. Only the truly memorable ones stick. So, you already have lots of gaps. I will just be filling some of them."

"Lozen, I ... I can't do this. I won't!" I tried, overcome by panic.

Director Toriq just sighed. "Look, I believe I've been very reasonable with you. I could have just threatened to kill your mother, but I didn't. However, if you try to back out of this now, I can have her dead by the end of the day. Just like Sora."

I just sat, breathing hard, with my mind spinning.

After a few seconds, Lozen said, "Well, let's get started, shall we?"

Before we started the memory manipulation, Lozen recorded me talking through what I had agreed to, so she could play it back to me after the procedure. This she filed away.

Then it was time. I took a deep breath, dreading this more than possibly anything in my life. Of course, Lozen didn't provide me the same grace Aeon's doctor did by distracting patients from focusing on the memories that were about to disappear. While the older memories would simply be added to gaps already in existence, I knew my experiences since leaving MaxSec2, still so fresh in my mind, would be mostly gone soon. I would remember almost nothing of Aeon and the Eridanians after this. Worst of all, he was going to think I turned on him.

Despite knowing that I should think of something else, maybe a childhood memory, for example, I couldn't help but race through my experience since being released, thinking that maybe if I focused hard enough, I could resist this procedure. But I was wrong.

The feeling was unlike anything I'd ever experienced. I felt like my memories were being shrouded in a fog, one that got thicker and thicker until there was nothing left to see but a dull gray everywhere I looked. It was disorienting, like pieces of myself were being removed, and the effect made me feel lost. I began having a panic attack, gasping for breath and sobbing uncontrollably.

When she had completed her main work, she sat back, looking very satisfied. I tried as hard as I could to pull the memories I had only just held back from the abyss, but there was only emptiness, confusion, and a deep sadness. It was so much worse than anything I could have imagined.

Then, Lozen sat forward and said, "Well then, better get on to phase two. Time to say goodbye to our discussions from your time here."

I was too defeated to try the same failed tactic with these memories. I sat limp, empty, and broken as the memories from my discussion with Lozen started vanishing from my short-term memory.

She was just finishing the procedure when I heard yelling and energy weapon discharge from somewhere in the building.

"What did you do?" she snarled at me, locking the door.

"What do you mean?" I asked, having no idea how I got here or who this woman was.

We sat in silence, listening to the skirmish going on only a dozen meters away. Then everything was quiet. What the fuck was going on here?

"Good, good. I knew the guards would take care of any unwanted incursions. Let's finish up, shall we? I have a recording I need you to watch."

She was just turning back to the desk when the door blew off its hinges, smashing into the wall beside her.

Two Collections agents walked through the door, followed by Chief Gershom. The woman's face went from shock to outrage in less than a second.

"Chief Gershom, what is the meaning of this? You have no right to barge into my office!"

"Lozen Toriq, you stand accused of treason for your role in the Killwave murders. We urge you not to resist, as resistance will compel Collections to employ forceful measures." Chief Gershom's expression brimmed with fury.

"But here is your mastermind," said Lozen, gesturing to me. "I've just been doing some memory analysis, and as you will see, she's behind the whole thing! I picked her up just as she was about to kill one of the scientists behind the technology!"

"Director Toriq, we found evidence in your department's code base indicating that you stole memory-removal technology from Dr. Ellis, which you further advanced and used in the Killwave murders. Please come with us."

Lozen looked hard at me, before Collections roughly escorted her from the room.

Now Chief Gershom looked at me, concern written all over her face.

"I'm sorry," she said. "We came as soon as we could. What has she done to you?"

"What are you talking about?" I asked, voice ragged. "And where am I? Is Trace here?" I felt completely disjointed, I had a splitting headache, and my heart was pounding out of my chest.

Gershom's expression became worried. "He is ... but he can't talk right now."

"Let me see him!" I yelled, struggling to get up.

"Okay, but then we have to get you to a hospital to be checked out." The chief looked genuinely concerned for me.

Once Gershom had helped me up, I staggered out into a large room, immediately seeing Trace crumpled in a pile, while a paramedic tended to him. I rushed over to him and collapsed on his body.

"Is he going to be okay?" I asked the paramedic, tears streaming down my face, and struggling for breath. I realized my knuckles were white from clutching hard to his jacket.

"Yes," responded the paramedic. "He took a shot from an NID but will be awake soon."

"Freya, we need to get you to a hospital," said Chief Gershom gently, now right behind me.

"Give me a fucking minute!" I yelled, startling Gershom, who took a step back.

While sitting with Trace, my mind started racing, searching frantically for any inkling of how I had gotten here. But there was nothing, just some flashes of a man in a cave. How could something like this happen? Was I suffering from amnesia?

Then my mind started spiraling completely out of control. Images of discussions I had had with people I didn't recognize started appearing rapid fire in my mind. It was overwhelming, almost like my mind was trying to reject them, as a body would a splinter. I felt anxiety welling up more powerfully than ever before in my life. My heart was racing, and I was breathing shallowly, hand on my chest.

"Are you all right?" asked Gershom, holding my torso and staring at me, face full of worry. "I think you should lay down."

I began to do as she had asked, but just then, a sharp pain shot through my chest, and I felt the world falling away. The last thing I heard was Gershom screaming at the paramedic to get me to the hospital immediately, as I collapsed hard onto the floor.

...

I awoke in a hospital bed with Trace holding my hand. He had tears in his eyes. "Freya! I'm so happy you're awake. You had me very worried!"

"What happened?" I asked groggily.

He looked at the doctor in the room, who shook his head side to side quickly.

"Listen, the details will come in time, okay? Right now, you need more rest."

"Tell me what happened, Trace," I said, gritting my teeth and staring hard at him.

Trace sighed. "You had a massive panic attack, following a ... procedure."

"What procedure? Trace, tell me what the fuck is going on!"

Trace looked afraid, then despite the doctor's protestations said, "You figured out who was behind Killwave." I could tell Trace was trying to navigate whatever had happened very carefully. "And they manipulated your memories to make it seem like it was actually you. Those ... artificial memories wreaked havoc on your nervous system, and you had a severe panic attack, which led to you passing out. We ... had to clear out all of the memories that were implanted, to ensure it wouldn't happen again. It was just too much for your mind and body to handle."

I could feel anxiety starting to build. "How long ago was I released from MaxSec2, Trace?" That was the last time I could remember having continuous memories.

Trace paused, looking very uncomfortable about what he was going to say. "It was over two weeks ago."

I immediately started searching my mind, trying to find any idea of what I had done in the last two weeks, but there were only flashes of people I didn't know. I started to hyperventilate and felt my heart rate begin to climb quickly. I was overwhelmed by nausea and suddenly had a splitting headache. I heard the doctor yelling, "We have to put her back under right now!"

I felt a needle, and I was out again.

When I awoke next, Trace was still by my bedside, looking very sad. I was heavily sedated this time.

"I'm so sorry, Freya," he said, weeping. "I gave in to your persuasive nature, but I should never have put that on you so quickly." He reached out and held my hands.

"It's okay, Trace," I whispered. "I appreciate you treating me like an adult instead of a child." At that I gave a hard look at the doctor, who was still in his same spot.

I fell back to sleep, that short period of conversation too much for my frail mind to handle.

Over the next several weeks, Trace slowly got me up to speed with everything I'd forgotten (as much as he and Libra knew, anyway). Much of it he would only tell me when we were alone, since it would be very problematic for me if others found out. The reason he had these details, and not the entire CAD, was because of that conniving AI. It had performed memory analyses on both Lozen Toriq and me but had held back certain details, something that was definitely outside of its protocol.

I was very interested to hear about when and how it had gotten details about my own activities, which Trace explained to me.

"As soon as you heard about Sora, your stress hormones went through the roof, and Libra began live monitoring your visual and auditory data, plus performing a memory analysis from your time after you went underground until you had your antenna repaired. Before you got zapped by Lozen's agent, we were able to run a facial-recognition scan and determine it was her that had taken you, which got us a search warrant to begin looking at the ITD Special Projects code base. We were able to use the decryption steps that Haidee showed you to find Sora's signature in the code specific to a secret memory-manipulation project they were working on. That got us the arrest warrant for Lozen."

Libra had also started live monitoring Lozen's visual and auditory data at the time I was taken, however, her office must have been equipped with some kind of jammer, because as soon as she entered the building, the ability to monitor her had ceased. However, as soon as she was arrested and removed from the building, Libra had been able to start a memory analysis of my time with Lozen, plus her overall involvement in the conspiracy since the beginning.

"So, what exactly does CAD not know about my activities?" I whispered, concerned about being charged with treason because of my cooperation with Aeon.

"Libra told Gershom it wasn't able to do a memory analysis of your time after release from MaxSec2, since Lozen erased that whole period," Trace said. "It also removed any parts of your conversation with the director that covered said topic."

Well, I may just be in the clear after all.

"However, it's not all good news," continued Trace. "The investigation into Libra has been handed over to the ITD, and they claim they are taking it seriously. Something about this not being the first time they've had allegations of rogue behavior." I just shrugged. Not much we could do about that. I just hoped Libra was up to the challenge.

After a long pause, Trace started telling me about the Somniacide ban. "An anonymous DD soldier sent a holo of some pretty distressing experiences to a few media outlets. The public outrage was intense, and the Somniacide was banned within two days. You wouldn't know anything about who made that holo, would you?" Trace asked, looking at me strangely. I just shook my head.

"So, what are they doing instead?"

"They've already started building a prison facility, far out from the city. What they are planning to do there though, is anybody's guess."

Chapter 10

"Junis, use more force when you push her upward!" I was yelling to one of my students, who was about twenty meters away.

"Apologies, Freya!" Junis called back, her peregrine falcon, Blaze, still clinging to her leather forearm gauntlet.

Despite the difficulties my students were having, the scene brought a smile to my face. About half of the dozen falcons and hawks were airborne, jockeying for space and peering around for any nearby prey.

I had started this all-women's falconry class about two months ago, and the demand had been surprisingly strong. The combination of being out in nature and learning to hunt with a badass companion (not me, their raptor), had been exciting for my students, and despite my somewhat terrifying reputation, in general they felt safe being out here in the wild with me watching over them.

I'd also started to get to know the students pretty well, with Junis being my favorite of the bunch. One of the reasons I liked her so much is that, like me, she was not your typical gregarious CiviLibran, but unlike me she'd learned to thrive in the environment, despite the challenges it presented her.

Junis worked from home as a part time naval architect, designing near-shore pleasure craft in all shapes and sizes. While some design work in core industries provided a guaranteed minimum CiVal score, this was unfortunately not one of them. Her schedule was at least pretty flexible, which allowed her to take up hobbies like falconry. However, for the most part, she spent her time alone, not really a great idea when the possibility of a CCC sentence was always looming over you. To combat this, she maximized her CiVal score during short and intense social bursts, such as acting as a deep-sea fishing vessel guide for large groups two days a week and singing at local clubs on the weekend. She had built up a lifestyle that provided her with a strong CiVal score of 3.8, while at the same time being something she could keep up sustainably without burning herself out.

It was relationships like this, and spending time out here, that had been crucial during my recovery.

Since leaving the hospital six months ago, my road to recovery (or at least, road to being able to function), had been very hard. Those first two months were the worst, as I had struggled mightily with what had been done to my mind. Even though I knew there was essentially nothing to remember from after my release from MaxSec2, I kept jumping to that period of time like a magnet, searching desperately for any glimmer of a memory. Instead, there was nothing, just a thick fog, one that seemed to trigger a predictable sequence of physical stress symptoms. It would always start with a racing heart, and shortly after that, hot flashes and sweating. The stress hormones released felt uncomfortable and relentless. It was like my mind was a storm, and I could not seem to form any rational thoughts whatsoever. I always ended up curled in a ball, sobbing as a pulsing headache and nausea overwhelmed me.

I was afraid to leave my apartment, for fear of an attack coming on while I was out. Unfortunately, by staying inside, consumed by my thoughts and the dread of another attack, I was caught in a never-ending loop of suffering.

It was Trace and my mother who had helped me start to break the cycle.

Coming over daily, they'd make small talk and tell old stories while

I sat, not saying much at all. Eventually I started partaking more, especially during stories about my father. It was nice to think about happier times, and most importantly helped me focus on something besides the feeling that I was permanently broken.

I'd always prided myself on my ability to deal with difficult situations, but going through this and finding it seemingly impossible to break out of the loop, I wondered if maybe I'd just been good at burying my problems very deeply.

After about two months, I got a surprise comm request from Lumi, my father's old workmate. She was boisterous as usual. "Freya!" she bellowed. "Don't you remember promising to come visit? What the fuck has been taking so long?"

I, of course, didn't remember saying that and told her as much.

"Ah, that's right, I heard that ITD psycho scrambled you up pretty good. Listen, we had a young goshawk slam into one of the shop windows here this morning. Poor thing broke one of its wings. I was wondering if you wanted to take a run out here and adopt the little peacock. Looks just like the one Damon used to have."

"Little peacock?" I asked, confused.

"Yeah, I'm assuming it was admiring itself in the reflection when it had the accident. Vain as anything, this beautiful little bastard is."

I couldn't help but laugh at that. "All right, I'll be out in a few hours. Is it with you now?"

"Nah, at the vet in town getting fixed up, but we'll go down and see it when you get here. By the way, how the hell do you tell if it's a male or female? There's nothing down there whatsoever!"

It felt good to get out of the city and was shocking to think that I hadn't done so in so many months. It was still winter, and the mountains had a nice covering of snow at the tops, framing The Bowl beautifully. I took my time and couldn't help but smile as I passed into my home valley. Despite not having lived there in decades, it still felt more like home than Novaluxia.

I met Lumi at the vet, hugging her for a long time before we went in. The little hawk was still heavily sedated to ensure it kept its bandaged wing from jostling around too much. It gave me a skeptical look, then closed its eyes and went back to resting. The vet told me it was a young male.

"What'll you call him?" asked Lumi.

"I think you're right; Peacock suits him just fine."

After we left the clinic, we headed back to Lumi's place, where some of my father's old work gang were already having drinks out by a fire. It was cold, but the fire was lovely, and I remembered how relaxing it was to warm your hands by a flame on a crisp winter's day.

It wasn't long before Lumi started telling her favorite Damon story, one I'd heard dozens of times before. Still, for whatever reason, it never seemed to get old.

"So, these two inspectors from Novaluxia show up at the plant, and of course, Damon just can't help but try and woo them, like he always did with city folk. Honestly, there was something off in that man's head. I'm sure of it." Lumi paused, making a placating gesture toward me. "No offense, dear."

"None taken," I said.

"It's a Friday, and Damon works on convincing them to stay overnight so he can take them up into the mountains the next day. They resist initially, of course, but he wears them down eventually, and they grab a hotel for the night, agreeing on the meeting coordinates before they part ways.

"Next morning, Damon heads up early so Whisper can do some hunting. The fellas show up while the goshawk is away, and Damon hangs out for a bit, shooting the shit. After about an hour, he starts wondering where the little hawk is, but wanting to surprise the guys, sneaks off without telling them where he's going.

"While he's gone, Whisper comes back, looking for Damon. Problem is, Damon ain't there, and instead there's two strangers in his place! Whisper goes ballistic, screeching and dive-bombing the fellas, probably thinking they killed his pal. One of the guys, scared shitless, stumbles backward, trips over a rock, and falls into the river!

"Now, Damon comes back right at that very moment and follows this guy down the river with the other inspector.

"When they finally catch up, he's on shore gasping for breath. He takes one look at Damon and starts crawling away, looking back from time to time with a terrified look in his eyes.

"Damon finally reaches him and asks what he's so scared of, and the guy, after staring wide-eyed at Damon for a few seconds, says, 'I always heard you rural folk were different, but no one warned me you were shape-shifters!'"

At that, Lumi and the others started roaring with laughter. I couldn't help but chuckle as well, even though I was quite sure the story was a *bit* embellished.

When Lumi offered for me to stay with her for a bit, at least until Peacock was ready to leave the vet, I accepted. Every day I went in to spend time with the little hawk, helping out with his rehab and getting him comfortable being around me. Of course, this also gave me lots of time to think about how unacceptable it would be to take him back to the city and live in an apartment. When I told Lumi this, she was so fast to offer me a more permanent solution, I knew she'd been just waiting for the topic to come up.

"Look, I'm at the plant all day," she said. "Plus, with the kids gone, you'd have the whole basement to yourself. And don't worry about rent; I'm just happy to have the company."

I'd ended up staying with Lumi for almost two months, rehabbing and training Peacock every day and getting outside as much as I could. Because of my condition, I was able to get a medical leave, meaning my

CiVal score stayed at one. That allowed me to take my time and focus on what was best for Peacock and me. Lumi had actually been the one to give me the idea about a falconry class, knowing my medical leave would eventually end. However, running something like that this far out from Novaluxia would have been doomed to fail, and plus, I was not seeing Trace or my mother nearly enough. So, I started renting my own place in The Bowl, near the foothills of the mountain range.

I had not broached the topic of Aeon's photo with my mother yet and wasn't sure I ever would. I suspected I probably discussed with Aeon whether he and my mother knew each other, but unless I were to ever see him again, I'd never know. To be honest, I was very reluctant to talk about that time, since it was mainly a trigger for more unpleasant feelings. Still, due to the success of my mother's photo-sending technique, we had established a similar type of code, just in case I needed to know more in the future.

"All right, everyone call your birds back, please!" I called out to my class.

When all the birds were back, I started looking around for Peacock. Just then, I saw a partridge burst out of the tree line, with my goshawk in hot pursuit.

"Class, watch and learn," I called out, pointing in the direction of the hunt. It was mere seconds before Peacock made the kill. The class cheered.

After we had said our goodbyes and everyone had headed home, I took a look up the mountain. I was going on my longest solo camping trip in well over a year, and I was excited.

I started hiking, and it wasn't long before the two topics that seemed to keep nagging me popped into my mind. While I hadn't spoken to Libra much at all since the hospital, mainly because of the investigation but also because it was just really bad company, I had been following along with what was transpiring. The investigation by CAD had unearthed more evidence of Libra performing unauthorized analyses, and the calls for reinitialization were getting louder. Fortunately, there were some strong voices on the other side of the aisle, who kept pointing out that the AI had only been doing what was in the best interest for CiviLibra. But still, it was definitely in danger.

The Somniacide ban itself was still in place, and so far, there had been no efforts to end it. There was now one war prison in operation, and the DD was claiming that it was working. However, I was growing suspicious that the reason behind wanting it in the first place was to allow for more thorough interrogations and possibly even memory analyses to be performed. And since the EdgeKind were mainly nonaugmented, that would require a surgical procedure to allow for access to the brain.

As for Trace and me, it was becoming increasingly apparent that if the ITD was able to break through the self-preservation measures Libra had put in place, it would only be a matter of time before our own activities were exposed. This had been a major cause of stress for us both, and at a time when I was just starting to recover.

Still, having no idea what was coming, or when, we'd agreed that maybe some time away from it all would help clear our heads for a bit before shit hit the fan.

After I'd hiked for about ten kilometers, I arrived at the same spot my where father and I had camped, way back when I was just a kid. It was also where his ashes had been scattered. It was spring, so there was not much foraging opportunity. Therefore, I'd brought more ingredients from home than I normally would. Tonight, I'd be recreating the dish I fondly remembered having with my father, albeit with purchased mushrooms, pine nuts, and garlic, to go along with Peacock's partridge.

As I was cooking, I got a comm request from Trace, who was camping a few kilometers away with Durant. He'd explained the surprise camping trip, quite out of the ordinary for him, as a test to see if he and Durant would be compatible living together full time. When he'd told me the plan, it'd taken all my strength not to mention they were basically living together already and had been doing fine. Still, I was happy he was going to have some time to relax. His new job, and the investigation, had him drinking like a fish.

"Freya! Where's that little feathered dragon of yours? He better not try and eat my Mochi!"

"I think you're imagining Shadow of Death, Trace. Peacock is probably a twentieth the weight of Mochi."

"Hey, why don't you hike over to our campsite tonight for a drink," Trace kindly suggested. He'd been doing everything in his power to make me feel included, and I couldn't express how grateful I was. Part of me wondered if maybe he thought of me like the sister he'd lost, but I'd never ask him.

"I appreciate it, Trace, but I think I'll lay low tonight. Maybe tomorrow?" I really liked the idea of him being so close by but wanted to be alone tonight.

"Of course, anytime that works for you."

That night, while sipping from a bottle of whiskey and stroking a sleeping Peacock, I thought about how far I'd come since the hospital and how it was the first time I'd felt more or less complete since the incident with Lozen. While my future was far from certain, and my recent past was a hot mess, that only seemed to make this moment all the more special. I felt close to my father out here, and though I had never considered myself spiritual, couldn't help but feel like I was part of something bigger, something far more important than the human drama I so often found myself tangled up in.

In this moment, I was at peace.

About the Author

Gavin Noble Mills is an engineer by trade and a dreamer at heart, seamlessly blending logic with the fantastical in both his profession and writing. He resides in Halifax with his wife and two spirited daughters.

Thank you for reading *Harmony's Betrayal*. If you enjoyed Freya's journey, I would greatly appreciate a review on Amazon—it helps other readers discover this story.

To stay updated on future releases and get access to behind-the-scenes content, sign up for my newsletter at:

Subscribe to my newsletter:

✉ https://subscribepage.io/Hgt1wv

Manufactured by Amazon.ca
Bolton, ON